THE
GIRL
IN THE
BOX

Books by Ouida Sebestyen

Words by Heart
Far from Home
IOU's
On Fire
The Girl in the Box

Ouida Sebestyen

THE
GIRL
IN THE
BOX

Joy Street Books

LITTLE, BROWN AND COMPANY

Boston   Toronto   London

First edition

The characters and events portrayed in this book are fictitious. Any similarities to real persons, living or dead, are coincidental and not intended by the author.

Library of Congress Cataloging-in-Publication Data
Sebestyen, Ouida.
   The girl in the box.
   Summary: Kidnapped and left in an underground room, Jackie explores her psychological strengths and limitations as she tries to make contact with the outside world by writing messages and sending them through a slit in the door.
   [1. Kidnapping — Fiction.   2. Survival — Fiction]
I. Title.
PZ7.S444Gi   1988   [Fic]   88-12849
ISBN 0-316-77935-0

                    10   9   8   7   6   5   4   3   2   1

        Joy Street Books are published by Little, Brown
                    and Company (Inc.).

                              FG

            Published simultaneously in Canada
        by Little, Brown & Company (Canada) Limited

            Printed in the United States of America

For my father

THE
GIRL
IN THE
BOX

IMPORTANT

If you have found this note in my pocket
and need to identify me, I am Jackie McGee.
My parents are Brian and Carol McGee,
301 East Hutto, Shickley Heights.

Notify them.

So it was just a dumb precaution, okay? A way to make sure people would know who they'd found, if Forget that. I can TELL them who I am.

It's weird, talking to myself like this on a typewriter. But the whole thing feels unreal. I am writing in the dark. In a cellar. Locked in. I think it's a cellar. I'm afraid to explore it yet. But I felt the walls in all directions, and it's small. The walls are concrete. So is the floor. I can't touch or see the ceiling. There are steps coming down. A heavy slanting door at the top.

I am trying to be calm and reasonable. I am all right. Not hurt or anything. But I am still so shaky I may not be hitting the right keys. I am waiting for this to be a joke. The door will open, a light will come on, people will laugh and let me out and explain what it's all about.

So I'm typing away as if this is something I do all

the time. Perfectly natural, right? That's why they invented touch typing, so you can do it in the dark.

But if this is not a joke

And nobody comes

Okay, so I've stopped and had myself a big slobbery cry. I'm better now. Fingers steadier. It's just that this has been a shock. Like suddenly falling flat on your face as you're just walking along.

I WAS literally walking along, and — wham! Primetime weirdness, all over the place. Too crazy even to be a dream.

Having it be a dream would sure be an improvement.

Anyway, the shock is wearing off. Nothing is happening. I can't just sit huddled on the steps. Don't I need to be doing something? Leaving more messages? Taking notes? Anything to keep my mind focused. At first I was so stunned, I couldn't do anything but stand here in the dark. Then gradually I felt my way up the steps and began to bang on the door and yell. "Hey, anybody out there? Hey, I'm down here. Anybody?" Sort of dazed uncertain stuff like that. Because I suddenly had the feeling that he was still up there, listening. It scared me. Do I want him opening that door?

But I had to start yelling again — other people might be right out there, actually passing by without knowing I was here. THEM I want! So now I yell every few minutes. Even if it brings him again, I'll take my chances.

But nobody comes, and I'm down here, wherever that is. I'm here by myself, locked in and so confused I'm not thinking straight.

What should I be putting down? It's sometime in the night. The rain was stopping about the time it happened. My hair is still damp. My shoes. I'm shivering, but not just from the cold. I've got to gather up my courage and feel all along the walls and floor again, and that door at the top of the steps.

Nothing like this has ever happened to me.

It's me again. Later. But I don't know how much later. I used to read stories about lost children who just lay down in the woods, bugs and snakes and all, and cried awhile and went to sleep. I used to think, "Not me, folks!" But I must have done it — right on the floor. Because I woke up and a wonderful thing has happened.

When I lean a certain way along the steps I can see a tiny slit of light showing along one side of this thick door. It isn't big enough to light up anything, and I can't get my head close to it, but it means there's daylight out there. Or at least an electric light has been turned on — something's changed. Even though it's still pitch-black in here.

My throat is raw from all the yelling, and I'm stiff as a board. Bruised here and there, feels like, but okay. I can't imagine what this really is and why it's happening to me. But for now I just want to stare at that little thread of light and think what it can mean.

TO ANYONE WHO FINDS THIS

My name is Jackie McGee.
I am close by. In something like a cellar.
Find me.
Please contact the police immediately.
So they can tell my parents I am alive.

DEAR MOM AND DAD,

The first thing is, I'm all right. Still dazed because it happened so fast. I guess April has told you everything she knows by now. He didn't hurt me, just shoved me around some when I tried to keep from getting into his van. But I'm okay so don't worry. Just find me and get me out of here.

This is so weird. It feels like I'm in a cellar. Remember when Gran took us to the farm where she grew up? What she called the cyclone cellar out in the backyard, with all the shelves of old canning jars in it? It's sort of like that, only smaller, I think. And empty — except for me. But it's a little concrete room with concrete steps coming down into it. So I'm sure it's underground. A bomb shelter, maybe? Can't tell in the dark. There's a heavy sort of slanting door. Locked. I can't budge it.

It's metal, I think. Do they put metal doors on cellars? Maybe it's an old door off of something else.

The important thing is that along one edge the door doesn't quite lie tight against the concrete, and there's a thin little seam of light showing. I'm going to push this letter through that little slot, so somebody can find it. Somebody will see it and take it to you. It's got to be morning out there now. I know you and the police and everybody are already looking for me. Somebody will see it. I'm yelling, too. I get as close to the crack as I can, sort of lying along the steps to get my face near it, and yell my head off.

We drove a long way. But I don't know if it was straight out of town or circling around, because he pulled some kind of grungy pillowcase thing over my head.

When he made me get out of the van we walked across what felt like weeds, and went around corners and stepped on crunchy stuff that was like gravel. Then he said, "Lift your foot up over that edge and start down the steps." I began fighting and screaming so hard he grabbed my shoulders and pushed me down really fast to the bottom and gave me another shove out into nowhere. I guess that was so I couldn't get my bearings fast enough to try to follow him up the steps before he could get out and slam the door down on top of me.

I'm trying to remember it moment by moment so I can tell it clearly. It's all still a jumble. I remember parts of it fine, but chunks are missing.

I can't remember what sounds he made locking the door. Maybe he dragged heavy things on top of it. I was busy trying to untape my wrists and tear that cloth thing off my head. But when I did, I was still in the dark. All I could do was grope around until I found the steps and crawl up until I could touch the door. It wouldn't budge. I hit it, and felt around it, and pushed and tried to find hinges or a handle. It's just a solid, heavy piece of metal at the top of the steps that won't let me out of this hole.

I sure could use you, Daddy. Maybe you'd know mechanical things to try. Leverage stuff. All I can think to use is my fingernails.

I don't know if there's some kind of little grill or vent in the roof for air. I can't reach high enough to find out. No light comes in. But I can breathe all right. So no problem there. It scared me at first, when the door slammed down. But the air is okay. Better than inside the pillowcase.

When I got brave enough I began to feel along the walls, scraping my feet along the floor at the same time. I hit something. I was so unnerved I just stood there, waiting for it to move or make a sound. Nothing happened, so I touched it with my foot again, and finally I got the courage to reach down and feel it. It was the typewriter. And farther on was my backpack. I guess he'd thrown them down into the cellar when he left me tied in the van and went to open the door. I guess he was making sure nothing of mine was left behind to look suspicious.

I couldn't believe it. I don't know why I kept hanging on to the typewriter for dear life while he was forcing me into the van. Yes I do — I was trying to hit him with it. My backpack had slipped down to my elbows — I remember he grabbed it off the rest of the way as he

10

was taping my wrists to some kind of handle in the back of the van.

Are you ready for what I had in the backpack? Typing paper. No kidding. A ream of it. Oh, other stuff, too. Lipstick. Comb. One earring. Just the kinds of things you need to blast through concrete walls.

Then I groped farther into a corner and found something else. A big jar that sloshes. I thought, oh great, is it water or is it kerosene or antifreeze or insect spray somebody's storing down here? I sipped a tiny bit. It tastes like water. Greasy or old, or something. I'm scared to try it again right away. Better wait and see how I react. There's a pile of bakery stuff, too. It feels like bread and donuts, coffee cake, things like that in plastic wrappers. With my luck it's probably all low-cal.

This is so crazy. It has to be a joke. A ridiculous mistake of some kind. If I'm not dreaming this, maybe it's a delusion I'm having from accidentally getting hit on the head or breathing something toxic. I try to laugh. I say out loud, "Okay, now. The joke's gone far enough."

I have to keep laughing, because the second I stop, all I can think of is that somebody fixed this place up for me. With plans for leaving me here, and keeping me alive. Somebody knew I was coming. Or if not me, the somebody I was mistaken for. I keep laughing, but it's getting harder. This has gone way beyond far enough.

I've explored all the walls and the floor again, inch by inch, like they do in movies. Only I poked everything with the comb before I touched it with my fingers. The movies don't show how frightening it is to slide your hands around in the dark, not knowing what you're about to touch.

The trouble is, nothing's here. The walls are plain, the floor has a tiny kind of drain or something, a round piece of metal with slits I could push the comb through. Down to solidness, like gravel. Maybe some kind of pump or machinery used to be in here. I can't guess. Could be one of those survival nuts poured himself a little hide-away where he could sit out a nuclear war, eating canned crackers and polishing his guns.

You'll just have to look for anything that could possibly be this place. I think it's outside, on a farm maybe, but it might be part of a factory or big warehouse or junkyard. An old military base? Airport? I don't even like to think of all the places it could be. I just know there was some kind of mix-up and I got left here, and you can straighten it out and find me. You're coming. I'm really calm now. Not scared. Just furious at the scumball who did this to me. I don't mean he did any-thing — not what you're probably thinking — so don't go all crazy, imagining things. He just dumped me down here like I was something he was storing for a while. But shooting's too good for him — he's sick, or whoever put him up to this is sick. Find out who — they've got to pay for this.

I hope you can read what I'm writing. I'm not the greatest typist. Fast, not fancy. The typewriter works, as far as I can tell, but I don't know if the letters are printing. I think I can feel little dents. It would be awful if I'm only writing invisible words.

I keep pounding away, because I don't want to stop and push these pieces of paper through that little slit up there. What if I push them out and they just drop into weeds or blow off into a ditch? How will they ever get to you?

I'm sorry — I know I'm going on and on like people who give you their whole medical history when all you did was ask, "How are you?" But it's like — as long as I'm writing, you're listening. I know that's dumb. I wish I could be giving you something solid to go by — where I am and why I'm here. I know you must be worried sick by now. You've probably questioned April over and over. Maybe even Zack, too. Thinking of you talking to them about me seems strange after what happened. But I guess all of you are trying as hard as I am to make some sense out of this.

Someone will find this letter and take it to you. I know you'll get it, and be relieved that I'm okay. Then you'll put all these crazy clues together and come looking for me. But hurry, will you? I feel so helpless, sitting here in this box.

Love,
Jackie

TO ANYBODY OUT THERE

I am in what feels like a cellar or underground room, with a heavy slanting door. Maybe with heavy things piled on it. This paper you have found should be lying right beside it. If not, try to calculate which way the wind might have blown it. Please call the police immediately. My name is Jackie McGee. I am the girl who disappeared. Listen to the news. See if other pieces of paper are scattered nearby. Maybe if you yell really loud I can hear you and yell back.

I am not making this up. Please help!

TO THE SHICKLEY HEIGHTS
POLICE OR LAW OFFICIALS

Or anyone looking for me.

I am Jackie McGee.

I am sure my folks have already told you I am missing.

On TV, when the police rescue people, don't they take their statements about what happened? I see it on the news, or in the documentaries I watch. So I am going to begin my statement, even before you get here. I need to stay busy. I need to straighten out things in my head.

I will explain what has happened as carefully as I can.

Do you need more facts about me? My parents are Brian and Carol McGee at 301 East Hutto, Shickley Heights. I am female — my real name is Jaclyn. I am five feet four, shoulder-length brown hair, hazel eyes. Just ordinary looking. Need to lose about ten pounds. I go to Dupree High School. No real enemies that I know of. No real friends, either. But that's a personal matter that has nothing to do with this stupid situation I'm in.

It started with April, though. April Beckner. It started with her coming to my house, last night. I think last night is what I mean. I can still see the little slit of light that shows along the edge of the door, so it must be Friday, now. It was Thursday evening when I came home late from school and she was in my room grabbing all her things up. We had been friends so long — eight years, back since I started to school in town — that half her stuff was at our house. Clothes that we exchanged back and forth. Books, records, tapes, all the things we had borrowed and shared and just thought of as "ours."

I didn't notice the exact time I got home. About the time it began to rain, because I had to run the last couple of blocks. I had stayed after school really late, helping backstage, and as I started up our walk I saw her through my window, holding stuff in her arms. I went into my room and stood there looking around at all the empty spots where "our" things had been. She'd snatched them from all over. My closet. Off the walls. Stuff she wasn't taking was thrown around. Like she was furious.

I guess I blurted out some really bright question, like "What's going on?"

She just opened a drawer and took out some belts and scarves.

I said, "Hey, you don't have to sneak in and steal back your stuff just because we're not friends anymore. I'll dump it out on the sidewalk for you."

April looked at me with those flat, glazed eyes that meant her mind was made up. She said, "I just want what's mine." She picked up the music box Zack had given us together, with the two little ceramic clowns on it.

I said, "Wait a minute. That's half mine! Don't you think we ought to talk about how — "

She glared straight into my eyes, opened her fingers, and let the music box drop to the floor. Little broken heads and arms flew off in all directions. "No, I don't think we ought to," she said. "Keep it. But that's the last thing we're ever going to share, Jackie. You're not going to interfere in my life like that anymore!"

Then she ran out, right past me, with her crushed-up clothes still on hangers. I couldn't move. Or think what to do. She had been angrier than I had ever seen her. And I didn't know why.

It was dark-looking by then, because of the rain. I guess my folks were getting groceries. If they had been home they wouldn't have let it end like that.

I noticed the typewriter on my desk. It was a portable we had bought together at a garage sale, pooling what money we had on us when we saw it. I don't remember who paid the most because it hadn't mattered then.

Since I was going to write the plays, and April was going to star in them, the typewriter more or less stayed at my house. But that didn't mean it was mine or that I wanted it. Especially now after what she said about sharing. Maybe to her it was part of the "interfering" she'd accused me of. And the paper, too. Last year she'd brought over a whole ream of typing paper — still in the box — that she'd sort of borrowed from her dad's office. He's a lawyer, and she said he had tons. I hadn't thought much about it, then. But I definitely couldn't keep it now. I shoved it into my backpack, and zipped the typewriter into its carrying case. I could be as cold as she could about who was messing up whose life.

I still had on my raincoat. I yanked up everything and started after her. She was way down at the end of the block, wobbling along, almost running, with her arms full of loot.

When my folks moved in from the country, April lived at the top of the hill in Crestview Estates, and our house was at the bottom of the hill behind it. Actually that made us just two blocks apart, close enough that we practically lived at each other's houses. But after my folks had to move to the dinky little place out on East Hutto, they, or sometimes April's dad, always drove us. She still didn't know that part of town too well, walking. So there she stood at the curb, probably trying to pick the shortest way home. She didn't see me. I could have yelled, I guess. I could have stopped her. But after what she did to the music box I just wanted to catch up and silently hand her the typewriter and paper, acting just as right-and-wronged as she was acting.

If I called her name she might think I was begging her to stop and explain things. I had done that too many times already. As often as I'd run after her to apologize for things I hadn't done.

She started off again, going straight through a puddle instead of around it. Like she might still be furious. Or crying hard. A block farther on she cut across a mall parking lot. The rain got thinner, but it was dark from lateness by that time. I may have even passed the van. I'm not sure. I'm trying to tell you everything, because some little detail might be a clue you can use.

I walked as fast as I could, trying to get closer. But I still couldn't make myself call to her to stop. April can mix people's feelings up. Mine anyway. I guess what I really wanted was to look tired and wet and put-upon when I handed her the typewriter and paper.

She passed some stores that were already closed for the night. Then she turned off on a narrow empty street I had never been on — I can't tell you the name of it. I was about the width of four lawns behind her when a van came up behind me, and passed, and parked in front of a building up ahead. I don't know one make from another, it was just a normal-looking wet grayish van that I barely noticed. I was really thinking that pretty soon I'd start to look stupid, following April halfway home in the rain just to make what she was doing seem shabby.

So I swallowed my hurt feelings and yelled, "Hey." She looked around, and stopped. She didn't start back toward me. She just waited, wiping either tears or rain off her face with one wrist.

Suddenly she called out, "What are you trying to do — get me as mixed up as you've got him?"

19

Her voice was so bitter I stopped in my tracks. She wasn't making any sense. "Mixed-up?" I repeated. "I haven't mixed him up — I haven't seen him."

"You must have!" she yelled. "He wouldn't be acting crazy like this if you hadn't worked on him! Do you like ruining people's lives?"

I just stood there, dazed. How could she expect me to answer a question like that? I said, "Whose lives? You got what you wanted!"

"No — YOU got what you wanted. He's dropped out of school." She sort of fired the words back and forth across me like I was a target she was trying to hit with a machine gun. "He's leaving. Do you understand? He says he can't handle what happened. YOU had to put that idea into his head!" I guess I took a step closer because she drew back and said, "Quit following me, Jackie. Stay out of my life." She wheeled around and began to run.

I started after her. I had to catch up and finish this. She passed the van. I was going by it with my eyes glued to April, trying to figure out what to say to her, when all of a sudden the door next to the sidewalk opened, and a man was standing in front of me.

I ran right into him. He grabbed me. I guess I automatically gasped, "Sorry!" because I thought I had nearly totaled him. But I hit his hand, too, trying to pull free. His grip broke, and I ran a few steps, jolting my backpack down to my elbows. I saw April stop and turn around, looking puzzled. Then he caught me again and shoved me forward, and before April knew what was happening he had grabbed her arm, too.

Her mouth opened to scream, but he just knocked

the breath out of her by smashing her against me. All her belongings flew out of her arms and she went veering off through a hedge into somebody's yard. I remember swinging at him with the typewriter, but he caught me and dragged me back to the side of the van and stuffed me in. Like he was some kind of dog-catcher. I couldn't believe it was happening. He yanked the typewriter out of my hand and smashed the door shut from inside just as April came blundering back out onto the sidewalk.

He poked his face close to mine and growled something. All I could see were dark eyeholes in the ski mask he had over his head. No mouth talking. The slit must have been sewed together. No face. Just that muffled voice that I realized had warned me, "Don't make a sound — you can't win."

He shoved me to my knees, and all at once he had tape around my wrists and was taping them to a bracket thing in the van. April's face appeared at the window. She began to bang on the door, but the man slid into the driver's seat and took off.

Nobody seemed to be around, but he did this TV chase-scene anyway, screeching around corners like an idiot. I was toppling one way, then another, with no way to brace myself. The third time my head hit the door, I was so furious I yelled, "What kind of dumb-ass game are you playing! You let me out or you're in big trouble — my folks — the police —"

My heart almost stopped when he slowed down and pulled off the road. But it wasn't to let me out. It was to drag a heavy pillowcase or something over my head and tape it shut around my neck.

He whipped into traffic again. I braced myself on my knees, and made my breath go in and out slowly so I wouldn't panic. I could hear engine sounds growing and fading as we passed heavy trucks. Then he gradually slowed down. It felt like we even stopped for red lights. The streets got bumpy and full of potholes. Then they felt like gravel, even dirt. I didn't have a clue whether he had driven straight down a highway to another town, or had just muddled around on the beltways, and we were still reasonably close to where we started.

Finally he stopped, and opened the side door and took out the typewriter and my backpack, scraping them past me. I yanked on the tape, trying to pull free so I could bolt out the door. But in only a minute he was back. He cut the tape away from the thing he'd wrapped it around, and made me get out and walk in front of him. He forced me down some steps, into what feels like a cellar. With a heavy slanting door. A little concrete room.

I know it sounds silly, but I'm hoping somehow you'll recognize where I am. I ought to be right at the spot where you find this letter. But it could blow away, couldn't it?

I can see how hopeless this must seem. There's not much to go by, is there? I'm sorry if I got off too much on my own problems. But what April was yelling was nearly as big a shock as what's happening to me now.

April lives at Number Six, Crestview Estates. Her dad's a lawyer — maybe you know him. She may already have told you all this, and even remembered the license-plate number and other things I wasn't seeing. Or maybe she hasn't. I can't believe she was yelling all those things at me.

But I hope some of this will help. I'm sorry a lot of what happened is still blurred. The parts that really seem sharp may not be any use to you at all. I can't imagine what kind of mistaken-identity, crackpot-on-the-loose deal this will turn out to be when you get to the bottom of it.

Find the weirdo with the van. He had a knife. Don't tell my parents this, please. He didn't hurt me or anything. But he cut the tape loose with a knife. When I realize what he might have done, I get all clammy.

He's going to have to pay for every second of worry he's causing my folks. He shouldn't be wandering around out there. You've got to stop him before he does something really terrible to somebody else.

Or comes back for me.

A Statement for the Police
by Jackie McGee

TTM

I don't know what else to do. Who to write. I've put the letters out through that little slit. I've begged for somebody to walk by and see them. I've yelled, and pounded the door. What else? I've felt around and around the walls and floor. It's the same solid concrete, wherever I hit it.

So I guess I'm talking to myself again. That's what the "TTM" stands for. Sort of like the meditation that people do to calm themselves and get in touch with the universe or whatever.

I don't know what I'd be doing without the typewriter and paper. Bouncing off the walls, I guess. Just the busy feeling of rolling paper in, and typing something, as if I had homework, makes all this seem a lot less bizarre.

It's the silence that's getting to me most. Silence is

not something you hear a lot of, anymore. Or whatever I'm trying to say. I strain to hear sounds — footsteps, voices, something alive around here. Somebody driving a tractor. Cars going by. I lie as close to that little slit of light as I can, and try to imagine what's out there. A farm? Trees? Sunshine?

Or an old abandoned building with loose things squeaking softly in the wind? I try to smell what's out there. I yell and listen. I pound the door and listen. All I get back is the feeling of thickness all around me. The solidness of being in the ground.

I feel really jittery. I sit cross-legged on the floor, with my damp raincoat for a cushion and the typewriter on the bottom step. From here I can't peep up just the right way to line up the crack and see that little slit of light like a tiny gold wire, but I know it's there. My mailbox. My eyes keep going up to that spot because it's the only other thing alive in here, besides me.

I've gone through the backpack again. Found a dime, it feels like. Some scraps of paper and a paper clip.

Great for getting through metal doors.

Went through the pockets of the raincoat. There was a little note, I guess. Anyway a piece of paper folded five-sided the way April and I used to fold the notes we passed in school. I don't remember putting a note in my pocket, but it's been a long time since I wore my raincoat. April may have worn it last.

It's hard to dry out in here. My hair feels like a used bath mat. I rub my cold hands together and jump up and down. And I run back and forth like a hyper two-year-old, hitting the walls and going "Ooof!" I put the food and water up on the steps to be sure I don't run into it.

The food and water. That's the part I feel the strangest about. Somebody put food and water here. That means all this was planned. Arrangements were made, beforehand. There's stuff for no telling how long.

What is THAT supposed to mean?

Am I supposed to eat this junk? For days? How much water does a person need to drink?

Assuming that this is just ordinary water in the first place.

I've got to drink something soon. I've already had a little piece of Danish. Last month's, it tasted like. I'm not sure I want to spread everything out separately on the steps and find out exactly how many donuts, how many slices of bread. It would seem like — well, it scares me a little. It's as if I was going to BE here.

Well, I'm not. I've got better things to do. I've got to try not to think about things that might upset me. Got to tell myself that all this is no worse than getting stuck in an elevator. You just wait it out. You just go clickity-click on the typewriter, making your own soothing elevator music, until the door opens and you go home.

I guess I've started a journal. Just to keep, not to mail. Some of this would look really queer, coming out of a crack.

I've already decided what tomorrow's breakfast is going to be. Like when we visited Gran in the hospital and she was checking off the selections she wanted, on a long chart. Only I'm being twice as picky as she was.

26

BREAKFAST

Pineapple juice. Cold. In a glass glass, not plastic.

Homemade waffles with crushed strawberries.

Bacon. Maybe an egg.

Two glasses of milk. Make that three.

Lettuce. Don't ask why. Just bring lettuce.

I'd like the morning news on the telly, but keep it light. No disasters. Nice weather on the way.

Cars passing, in sunshine. I'm paying for this. I want sunny cars.

I'd settle for Mom plopping the cereal box down in front of me on her way out the door.

If I don't keep busy I think about him. I see those eyeholes, and know he's inside, looking at me. Seeing me from behind that mask, but not letting me see him.

Funny, I just burst out crying. Felt sort of silly when my nose began to run and there wasn't anything to wipe it with. Sort of let the dribble absorb on the knees of my jeans. I'm fine now. Except I just realized there isn't going to be any toilet paper in here, either, when I need it.

Okay, No-Face, you goofed. All this stuff to eat and drink — so where's the Porta-Potty? What about a mattress and a blanket? Get your act together, you weird bastard — this is ridiculous!

DEAR MISS FLANNERY,

Surprised to be getting a letter from me? I'm surprised to be writing you. But I thought, Why not? We can call it an extension of that little Let's Get to Know Each Other Better warm-up assignment you gave us the first day at school.

I was really excited that you're in on that combination History—Language Arts thing and I get to be in your class again. I really got a lot out of English last year. Thanks for being patient with me through all that. I really

I'm saying "really" too often. Why do I do that when I talk to you? I admire you so much and want to be articulate like you, but my tongue takes a plane and leaves my brain at the airport.

You said last year that writing about wizards and spies and kids with antigravity sweatshirts was fun but that my own life was definitely as interesting as any of that imaginary stuff and you'd like to see me write about what I knew about. I remember, because I spent a weekend trying to think of something I knew. I understand what you meant, though, so maybe I'll give it a try. Since I find myself — as they used to say in old novels — with a not inconsiderable amount of really empty time to kill.

MORE LET'S GET TO KNOW EACH OTHER
FOR MISS FLANNERY

Well, I was born in a city hospital, but we didn't live there — we lived in the country. We even had chickens. A long unpaved driveway went through the oaks to our house. In winter the smell of oak smoke got into everything, the rooms, the wash on the clothesline, the air at night. I loved it. I would run in the road at dusk, taking gulps of smoky air that smelled like home and happiness.

I started school while we lived there. My feet went to sleep every day during the bus ride. My mom said it was horrible, her baby standing by the bus stop in the sleet on dark winter mornings. That was when she began to talk up the idea of moving into town.

We didn't, though, until I was eight. I think that first half of my life was the best. Maybe not.

I'm about the youngest sixteen you can be. Book-smart, maybe, but pretty life-dumb. I could make good grades, but I don't, so how can I be intelligent, much less wise? For instance, I have a big vocabulary for my age, and yet I try not to use it anywhere I might sound like a show-off. I don't know if I'm a good writer. I won a prize for a Halloween story, and in a contest before that, I got a dictionary. I want to write plays and novels, and especially documentaries. But my life has been so EVEN. With my folks loving me and all that. Things haven't happened to me like they have to April and Zack. I've never had real troubles, or been stretched. Somewhere I read that a lot of times people think they've led a brave triumphant life, when what they've really been is lucky. I've been lucky.

April's the one with the full life. She's been to Hawaii and stuff like that. But some of the things she's gone through — I never know whether to laugh or cry. Her mom is one strange lady. She locked April's dad out of the house once for four days. Wouldn't open the door for anyone but the pizza delivery boy. Not even April — she stayed at our house, and lucky for her, she could wear most of my clothes. The first night, she and I went over and looked in through the windows to see if her mom was all right. She was watching TV and eating ice cream from the carton, so we didn't go back.

When April finally got in, her mom had given herself a new hair color and run up a three-hundred-dollar phone bill talking to some colonel out in Guam or somewhere. Not long after that he came back to the States and she left April's dad for him. I sort of liked her, but as my mom said, she was one poor excuse for a mother. She always seemed sad. You couldn't blame her, exactly — Mr. Beckner is mucho macho, really handsome and sharp. He jogs and works out and has this hard stomach you could slam racquetballs against. But he doesn't know how to talk to April, or be there for her.

He hit her with his coffee mug not long after he divorced Mrs. Beckner. I saw it, but I think he forgot what he had in his hand and meant to make a sort of authority gesture the way he does in court. He never did apologize to April. When she mentioned it once he just said he'd been "stressed" at the time. It left a little bump on her forehead.

Zack and April have been the most important people in my life. Well, my parents. But, you know. To talk to, to choose to be with and care about and share your days and secrets with. To trust enough to share your real feelings with.

For a long time I had mixed feelings about my name. Jaclyn was kind of odd and trendy. But Jackie made me sound like a nightclub comedian or something. A little boy. Then Zack changed how I felt. He began to play with my name.

I'd be out of school with the flu and he'd call up asking, "Is this Jackie O'Lantern, the lady who started the Chicago fire? I hear you're not feeling so hot today." I was glad he wasn't afraid to sound silly and nine years old. So I could, too. Especially when I was depressed and all crunched up tight with some kind of problem. Like, I'd say, I hate my ears — I look like Mickey Mouse. Zack and April would tell me to get real, I had perfectly good cute ears that were just right for my shape of face. But I'd say, what does THAT mean — my shape of face? And I'd go all hopeless.

April would roll her eyes and give up on me, but Zack would take my hands and say, "Okay, Jackie-in-the-Box, you can't stay in there." Then he'd pretend to wind the handle on one of those little tin toy music boxes, going,

31

"Doodle-dee doodle-dee," and squinching his eyes as if a lid might fly up to let a little clown pop out and startle him. Whenever he began winding and doodling, I'd have to smile in spite of myself. He could always coax the lid open.

I know it's dumb to spend so much of my life feeling low. I promise myself I'll do better, then something presses me down and I sit there, and something else presses me down tighter. Like my grades falling, or how I look — my ears, my shape, my mom saying, "If you want to lose ten pounds, lose it — don't just eat and moan!" My dad saying, "Good lord, her bones are sticking out already — don't tell her that." They've started arguing about everything. If one says yes the other one has to say no. And it's always me getting slammed back and forth like a tennis ball — how I'm doing, what I need — no she can't — why shouldn't she? I don't know how I'm causing all this anger between them, but I am.

This isn't working, Miss Flannery. It makes me feel very self-conscious. I'm saying personal things — cleaning out my mind the way I do my room, by dumping everything on the floor. I need to do more sorting before this can be a letter to anybody. I'm sorry.

Maybe what I ought to write for you is a story. With a story I could tell the truth if I wanted to, but you'd read it and say, "Is this real, or fiction?" And you'd never know. Maybe I'll do you a story.

Right now I've got to stop and yell, and eat something, because my arms are shaking. Besides, I've only got so much bright crispy ho-ho-ho left in me, and I used up most of that in the letter I wrote my folks.

The light is gone. I just now knelt on the steps like I've been doing, and tilted my head to line up the light — and it's not there.

I suddenly feel so let down. Tricked, by something I trusted. I know that's foolish. It's just dark outside. Or if this room is inside some junkyard or something, a light's been turned off. I've got to yell. I've got to pound. How could a whole day pass, and nobody come for me?

DEAR MOM AND DAD,

Hi, it's me again. It seems to be night but I'm not sleepy yet, so I took a refreshing but very short walk, ate a beautiful pasteboard coffee cake, and just thought I'd check in with you one more time.

I can almost hear you telling each other that I'm somewhere close and it's only a matter of hours before we're together again. The police are doing all those things they do in cop dramas — finding witnesses, questioning you and April and people at school, and Mr. Beckner, if they know where to look in Vegas. Even Zack.

Zack will be telling the truth if he says he hasn't talked to me, or seen me. This has been a long strange week. It's true I haven't spoken a word to him since Saturday at the lake. Every time he called I hung up when I heard his voice. I even cut some classes at school to stay out of his way. I didn't know how to handle it. I wish I could explain all this. But it's personal.

April said he's dropped out of school. I don't understand. Talk to her — find out what's happening. Before you got home, April came by and took all her things. That's why my room looks so trashed. She left our typewriter, but I didn't think I ought to keep it, so I ran after her, to give her custody for a change. I caught up over past the mall. I don't know the street, but the first house on the corner has a yard full of those huge tall sunflowers, if you want to tell the police. About the middle of the block was were the van stopped.

Please don't blame yourselves for any of this. Promise you won't. When we lived behind Crestview Estates, April and I literally wore a path between each other's houses, remember? Walking to meet each other to go to school, walking to sleep over, all that — and nothing ever happened. I know you're telling yourselves you should have been at home and it wouldn't have turned out this way. You'd have driven her home. But the person who should have been at home was her dad. He should have brought her over to get her stuff, instead of heading off on one of his starting-on-Thursday weekends.

I hope they told you in a careful way, so you didn't think something really awful had happened to me. I hope April didn't go into one of her productions. She may have had a big reaction when he snatched me and left her. You know, like a soldier realizing a grenade has just missed him and shredded his buddy. Maybe not. It's a weird feeling, not having any idea how she's reacting. I guess when you think about it she always did most of the acting, and I did the reacting — so this is a change.

She was saying some really surprising angry things just before this happened.

I wish I had more information to give you. But not much is going on down here. I've typed so long my fingers are claws, and I ache from sitting funny. How do the Japanese manage all this cross-legged-on-the-floor stuff? Or was that only in the old samurai days like that movie series at the library?

I keep thinking about the cellar in "The Wizard of Oz." Remember in that movie when the tornado's coming? Did you ever notice as they're closing themselves into the cellar that you can see light through the cracks in the door? I always imagined them down there ankle-deep in the rainwater that was pouring in. But I'd give them my good solid door in exchange for theirs, any day.

That movie always left me worried at the end, when everybody's back from Oz, changed to their real selves again. I expected Miss Gulch — the Wicked Witch — to ride up on her bicycle again and try to take Toto away forever. I was afraid the real life-and-death drama was just starting.

Guess what? I've actually typed myself so tired I'm willing to plump up my backpack pillow, get into my raincoat jammies, put my feet into the thing that was over my head, and try to rest awhile.

I wish I could see you. I wish I could let you know how alive and all right I am. I'm sorry you're going through this. Seems like all I can do is cause you trouble. Please don't be worried. I'm not worried. It's good to talk to you — or whatever I'm doing. Sending out the good thoughts. This is a crazy thing to be experiencing, but I'm telling myself it's merely a brain-boggling puzzle to solve.

I would have chosen to be marooned on a tropical isle, if I'd been given a choice, but being in this place sure gives me time to think. I've never in my life had so much uninterrupted time to think. Don't be surprised at any odd thoughts I'm passing on to you. Things look different from down here.

I hope everything is going well, and the clues are falling together. It's hard to be patient, but any time now I expect to hear that door being pried open, and voices shouting my name.

Love,
Jackie

TTM

The light is back! Is it morning? I woke up so cold I was curled up like a pill bug with my knees practically stuck to my nose. I gradually got unrolled and climbed up to look — and there it was. I hope I haven't slept so long that it's noon and I've missed half my daylight. It doesn't change the blackness in here, but it lifts my spirits to be able to get in just the right position and see that little gold streak glowing. I put my hand up to it, as if I thought I could feel warmth.

I'm really shaky. I had to eat again, and take a drink, before I could crawl up out of my gloom. I feel as dark inside myself as this little room is. I try to exercise. Back and forth, back and forth, like a zoo tiger. Hand hit wall, turn, three steps, hand hit wall, turn. Now I know why they have those haunted eyes.

At least they see. In here my fingers have to be my

eyes. They look and look at these grainy walls, the dirty floor with the little drift of leaves in one corner, the food, the water jar, the backpack. I even touched a spiderweb. It scared me, not to know if I'd disturbed a spider or just reached into an old discarded web. I like spiders. In the light. But now I don't want to go into that corner. My stupid imagination says things are crawling on me. I keep shaking out my raincoat and the pillowcase thing. I rubbed my donut. Didn't want to crunch down on anything I wasn't expecting.

What's the matter out there? Why isn't somebody doing something? It's been a day and two nights, according to my little light. How much longer do I have to wait? I can't work this out by MYSELF. I know I've got to stay reasonable. This has to have a reason. I have to look at all the possibilities, really calmly. All of them.

A mistake. That happens. So what's the worst it could be? He thought I was someone else. Somebody he wanted? Somebody he was hired to carry off? Somebody important?

Am I kidnapped, for heaven's sake? Like for a ransom? Why? My folks don't have money. Nobody wants to get even with them. Or exchange me for anything.

It's too farfetched. But so is any other explanation I can think of. Did somebody dare him to grab the first person who came by? Did he dare himself, like those boys in that Clarence Darrow trial who just picked someone at random to murder? Hey, I'm not thinking that — it just popped into my head as an example. I'm only trying to figure out if he was stoned or sick or drunk or sadistic or crazy or what. Did he think he was getting orders from God? Was he just desperate for money? Then why didn't he think it out and snatch somebody rich and able to pay his price?

Even grabbing April would have made more sense than me.

If he's mentally ill, that's different. But if he did this for money, to pay for drugs or something stupid like that —

I never felt this way about a person before. It's hard to make him real — someone with a name and a past and a favorite flavor of ice cream. All I'm getting right now is a big hot blur of hate.

THIS LETTER IS FOR APRIL BECKNER
IN CARE OF BRIAN MCGEE,
301 EAST HUTTO, SHICKLEY HEIGHTS

I figure you're there. If your dad was already on his way to Las Vegas when it happened, you must have called my folks. If they were home by then, they naturally rushed to get you. Anyway, I picture you staying at my house, if your dad's not back yet. Or even if he is. I picture you at the center of whatever's going on.

It's not easy writing to you, April. I feel like I'm — what do you call it — fraternizing with the enemy. I have really bitter feelings. Or maybe it's more like humiliation, to need to keep talking to you, even after what we've been through. But turning to you was always the first thing I thought of, all these years, when I had to talk. So it still seems natural to start pouring everything out, as if nothing had changed.

41

I'm not going to dig around into what happened. I just want to stay very civil and unemotional. So consider that I'm just doing out of habit what I always did — right up until that moment at the lake when everything broke to bits.

Look — I've got the typewriter.

After all those blocks, in the rain, catching up to give it to you. And the paper — that's definitely not mine. But when he threw me in the van, somehow the backpack and typewriter came with me. Wasn't I trying to crack his ribs with it?

What kind of freak was he? He didn't say anything that would explain what he was doing. Just orders. "Get down," and stuff like that. "Shut up." I guess I was yelling a lot of things back at him.

Tell my folks I'm all right. They must be going nuts.

I'm locked up in a cellar or someplace underground. You know how I feel about changes — about staying nice and safe — boy, am I safe. It has a metal door, and steps. Didn't Miss Flannery say someone thought "cellar-door" was the most beautiful word in the English language, or something like that? No way. Not as beautiful as Outside, Backhome, Hotbath, Realbed.

I can't get over how unreal this is. I guess you're okay. You were pounding the side of the van the last I saw of you.

There's a little place where the door and the cement don't touch. In the daytime I can see a faint little slit of light. I'm pushing messages out. To my folks and the police. To whoever might be out there. I know. It's weird. But wouldn't you? It's something to DO. I have to keep thinking I'm still in control here.

At first I thought all this was some kind of crazy mix-up. Mistaken identity, or some little looney who wiggled out of his straitjacket and started acting out his fantasies. But I have food and water in here. Just as if someone meant to keep me plump and juicy for a ransom or something. Why? It's bizarre. It doesn't make sense.

I yell and bang. Nothing. I try to feel vibrations, like a lot of cars leaving a factory at quitting time. Machinery being turned off or on. Anne Frank in the Secret Annexe, and all that. I pretend I'm a spy observing everything so I can put it in my report. I try to imagine what kind of documentary this would make. What kind of play. A one-woman show, it would have to be. A One Really Shook-Up Girl show.

Actually I'm staying very cool and on top of this. Especially to my folks.

At first I wasn't sure what he left was water. But it is. Awful, but water. The jar is so big and heavy I can't get a grip on it. When I tried to fill the lid, so I could drink from it, water dribbled down. I don't dare waste a drop, so now I cradle the jar in my lap and sort of boost it up so I can tilt it and drink that way. Goes great with the petrified bread.

The worst thing is that my sleazy little hotel suite doesn't have a bathroom. Yesterday I waited till I nearly exploded. Finally I used the drain. There's this little kind of grid in the floor, not connected to a pipe or anything, just to let any drainage go down into some gravel. So you could say this whole room is a big potty you can't flush. The drain won't work for the solid stuff, though. Can you believe taking a dump in an empty

43

donut box? The smell in here is beginning to be super-gross. I've got the box in a plastic bread wrapper, way off in the spiderweb corner. Guck. What I wouldn't give for a lovely huge coffee can with a plastic lid.

Saying there's light up there isn't really accurate. It's just a thin line of difference from the rest of the darkness. I hold what I've written up to it, but it doesn't light up the page, so I'm not sure if the ribbon is marking words on the paper. I can feel little dents on the back, but what are they saying? I hope I'm hitting the right keys. If I'm not, all this is going to look like the squiggly notes I jot down at night when I get an idea for a story or poem.

This little slit of difference came, then went away, and came again, so I guess it's recording day and night. My clock. I guess each time I see it I should scratch a mark on the wall with something. But wouldn't that be worse, knowing whole days were passing? This way I can tell myself, hey, it just SEEMS long without TV.

But why am I talking about days? I am going to be out of here, today. This day.

I believe it, every time I stick another little sheet of paper out the slit. I'm so grateful for the typewriter and paper. I'd have gone bonkers without it, really. As long as I can whack away like a drunk woodpecker at whatever wiggles in my brain I can keep going.

April, why were you taking all your things from my room without telling me or my folks? Why did you run out so suddenly, like I had a contagious disease? What kind of fever were you in? We could still have acted civilized.

You broke the music box on purpose.

I couldn't understand half of what you said. Are you sure you knew what you were saying? Partly I was running after you to make you stop and explain. Especially that part about Zack leaving. But then we crossed the path of some no-face creep in the rain — and now I have different questions to ask.

Was the ski mask purple? How horror-movie can you get? Imagine, a ski mask on a warm September night. He was just taking special precautions not to look conspicuous in a nice blue-collar neighborhood, right? What a no-brain. I sit here thinking of him put away forever, staring out at the world through iron bars instead of purple eyeholes. No. Staring out into the dark, so he'll know what it's like.

This could be crazier than it seems. He may have mixed me up with someone else. So some rich wheeler-dealer with a teenage daughter may be getting ransom notes saying, "If you want to see your daughter again —" when she's standing right there and her father doesn't have the foggiest idea what's going on. While my folks are asking each other if I could have run away with some creep in a van. Or be in trouble. Asking why I didn't talk to them about it.

Tell them I don't understand this any more than they do. I didn't run away. I wouldn't hurt them like that. If they ask about you and me and Zack, tell them we were going to work things out. Make them believe it — telling one more lie won't hurt you.

April, could your mother have planned this? I know it's farfetched — but could she?

What if she wanted you back — could she want you to come live with her and Colonel Wargames, whatever his name is? So she hired this hit guy to grab you, and he goofed and got me. Then when he realized what he'd done, he panicked and didn't dare contact her again. Maybe she's trying to squeeze money from your dad. Or just for spite, after the hard time he gave her with the divorce.

Find out from her! Even if you did swear never to speak to her again. You've got to check this out, no matter what you feel personally. I don't belong in here.

Sorry. Bread-wrapper time. Disgusting. A full plastic bag is going to be a gift to that freak — whammo, right in the face — if he ever opens this door.

No, I guess not. If he ever opens this door I'll be saying anything in the world to make him stand aside and let me go up those steps.

It's cold down here. I stay wrapped in my raincoat a lot. I don't know how much water to drink or bread to eat. Or how to divide it out. I count it and stack it, and it falls out of the wrappers onto the floor, and I'm on my knees gathering crumbs. How careful do I have to be? The bites ball up in my throat when I think about coming to the last piece. Then I get even more scared thinking he might come back to pitch more down those steps. I can't decide what to do to be prepared or in control.

I should just keep writing hard, I guess. At least my MIND isn't stuffed into a pillowcase. I can do something more creative than claw the walls.

But I hate to think he's brought me to a closed-up warehouse or old military base or someplace out in the boonies where nobody comes anymore. I'm afraid to go to sleep and not know if I've catnapped a few minutes, or blacked out for some reason and a long time has passed. I'm even scared I'll wake up and hear that door above me opening and see him looking down.

I found a metal lipstick in the backpack, and sometimes I undo it and practice jabbing the top half, with the sharp edge out. I could use it. I really could. Right into those shadowy eyes.

I'm okay, though. I feel better now, just from talking the way we used to. You were always a good listener. At least you nodded and grinned at the right places. I thought you were listening. You don't have to take this as a personal letter. I know things are finished between us and we can't be friends again. But I've always shared everything with you.

And thought you were sharing everything with me.

I wish we could have talked about what happened at the lake. I was thinking about it, just before I got home and caught you carrying off your things. I was hoping that, maybe if I explained why I reacted like I did, you'd explain why you did what you did.

But you yelled all that ugly stuff, and ran. And then all this happened. So we didn't talk.

I know we've had some real battles, with real tears, and sometimes we wanted to pull each other's hair out, but I think being able to talk, finally, every time, is what made it possible for us to stay friends so long. Being your friend is not something I can give up lightly.

I wish we could have talked.

For one thing, maybe I wouldn't be here now.

I need to stop. I'm tired. I've got to move around — my feet have gone to sleep. But I hate to end this. It feels like when we used to hang up the phone, you know? Click — and we were separated. We weren't Siamese twins breathing together, finishing each other's sentences and topping each other's puns. We were just two cut-apart things that had worked better when they were connected.

April, this isn't some wild idea you and Zack dreamed up, is it? Something that got out of hand, maybe? Okay, this is what's called getting paranoid. But who else, except you two, would want to hurt me?

I'm going to hang up, now. And mail this off to you at my little letter-slot.

April, why did you say I ruined people's lives? How could I do that?

TTM

I get so restless I don't know what to do with myself. I do jumping-jacks and jog in place, and I even tried reciting poetry out loud. But it's too eerie. In my mind I talk fast to myself about anything, the crazier the better, as if I were a grown-up trying to distract a whiny kid. Otherwise I'll fret, I'll get angry, I'll yell at the door, "Somebody open this thing! How long do I have to wait!"

So I ask myself questions. I interview myself.

Like, how do kidnappers know how much ransom to ask for? In dollars and cents, what would I be worth, for instance?

Not a whole bunch.

Except to my folks — they'd say I was worth more than all the money in the world, right? But they couldn't raise a ransom for me without some kind of help.

I think my mom expected wonderful things from

moving into town. My dad would have stayed in the country. But he came in. For her, I guess. For me. So I'd have "Advantages." Advantages are important to my mom. I'm really sorry they didn't agree with each other about where to live. Especially since my dad hurt his back so bad at work. On days when he can't go to Pee-wee's, I watch him lying on the couch staring at TV. His face looks puzzled, as if he's wondering how his life got this way.

Not long ago I mentioned that I liked our other house better. My mom thought I meant the house at the foot of the hill behind Crestview, when we first moved into town. But it wasn't that place I meant. I was wishing we still lived at our old house in the country, putting pans under the leaks in the roof. I was wishing we were having breakfast on the porch again, watching the grapes get ripe. And Gillie would still be our dog. I'll never forgive them for making me give him away when we moved to Shickley Heights, just because there wouldn't be a yard. Why couldn't we have made a fence? Or bought a different house! You don't hand a member of your family over to neighbors and just walk away.

I hope you're happy, Gillie. Remembering the good times we had together. But I hope you're not still wait-ing for me to come back. Being trustful can break your heart.

I still dream about you. The last dream I had, we were running in a field together. Your tongue was prac-tically streaming out behind you. I hope you aren't dead. But maybe you are, and the next time we meet we'll be two little balls of light, ectoplasm or whatever Miss

Flannery calls it, all changed, but finding each other again. You meant so much to me, Gillie.

Anyway, I still hold it against them. I'll never forget the helpless feeling of knowing THAT was going to be the way it WAS, and there was nothing I could do about it.

Sometimes I want to yell, It was all so stupid! Why did we have to move, anyway? I could have kept on going to that school. I didn't mind the bus. I might have found a teacher like Miss Flannery, and grown up intelligent and happy out there. Maybe happier.

All I would have really missed was having April in my life. And Zack, I guess.

My dad loved that piece of land. It had been his dream. My mom gave it a good try, as far as I could tell. But she just couldn't live that way. She had been a city girl. So they compromised, and came here to Shickley Heights, and nobody's happy. All they ever wanted was to make the best of things. For me. For keeping us together, whatever it took.

I wasn't much help. I was a real pain, in fact. A self-centered brat. When we moved into town, and April and I were starting to be friends, I felt really defensive about telling her what my folks did. I tried to make a joke about how my mother was going to school to learn enough to teach second-graders. I didn't want April to come to our house and catch my dad home from Pee-wee's Automotive, crashed out on the couch still wearing his hard-toe shoes and white socks, with "Brian" embroidered on his chest.

April was too special to risk losing.

Then one Saturday without any warning she stopped by on her bike. I walked into the kitchen and she was helping my mom scrub up something that had boiled over. The room was full of stinky smoke. I almost died. She stayed for lunch, and ate macaroni and cheese until she nearly popped. Before she left, my dad tightened her handlebars for her. And there we all were. Instant second daughter for them. Instant family for her. Instant lesson-learning for me.

Okay, Jackie — do your folks know you're grateful for all those things they've taught you and shown you? For being patient with you through all the learning? Did you ever try thanking them?

How did we get into this question-and-answer game, anyway? I think the TTM got off the track. But thanks for the interview, Miss McGee.

Anytime, Miss McGee.

DEAR MISS FLANNERY,

You must be thinking about me. Because just now you came into my mind, propped on the edge of your desk with your hands waving, conducting the whole class of us like a symphony. Parts of Speech in B flat major. You gave me that almost-smile of yours, the way you do sometimes when you need someone to share the weirdness with. I just sat here rigid, expecting to hear your voice hesitating over just the right word. All those great words! Mollycoddle. Transcend. Wretched. You didn't think I was listening, did you, those days I stared out the window?

I think you understand that it wasn't you or your class I was resisting. I loved your class. It's just school. I was afraid I was going to disappear into Dupree and never know what the rest of the world was like.

Or maybe what I was really trying to do was to get solid F's and stay in school forever.

Are you afraid of changes? Maybe you are — haven't you been at Dupree forever? A gray hair for every kid you tried to pound the love of language into, right?

I'm going to start the story I mentioned. This is being a long day. Please excuse the awkward spots. I can't go back and change words or rearrange sentences. You know I never liked to revise what I wrote — but honestly, I didn't get myself into this predicament just to get out of revising.

A STORY
by
Jackie McGee

He started school at mid-term. They discovered him in drama class, doing the scene in "Romeo and Juliet" where Juliet's cousin picks a fight with Romeo's friend Mercutio and kills him. He was Mercutio, all slender and quick. As they wandered around, half-watching, he suddenly staggered to the edge of the practice stage, mortally wounded, and took a fantastic, bone-splintering fall down the steps.

It got their attention. They gasped and started toward him, but he stood up, and his eyes, as intense as eagle eyes, locked on each of them before he walked away.

"Don't tell me," Amy whispered. "It's happened again."

Lynn only sighed, and nodded.

"It" happened regularly. One of them was given a ticket to something both of them would kill to go to. Or they both saw the only-one-in-their-size sweater in the store window at the same instant, and went through the same routine. You buy it. No, YOU get it. Or they both fell for the same boy.

Liking and wanting the same things was hard on the friendship. But most of the time they worked it out, by sharing the sweaters and letting the boys go their own ways.

His name was Josh, and he had cracked a rib in that dramatic death scene. When they found out, they baked him a cake and wrapped a wide strip of adhesive tape around it, to match his taped-up chest.

So, almost to their surprise, a three-sided friendship started. Without ever discussing it, they made a point of falling into a delicate balance, careful to treat — and like — each other equally, without breaking into a two-some that would leave the odd one out.

In February they went to a costume party as the Three Blind Mice, wearing little fake-fur heads with big ears, and huge dark glasses and funny little jackets and mufflers. They won first prize. But it was an album, so rather than try to divide it up they gave it to the ca-terer's boy who was cleaning up the mess after the party.

He said, "Thanks, meese. You're all right." And he looked at the three of them as if they were all one thing — not separate people.

The first test came when Josh was offered a ride in a sailplane.

"They said I could bring a friend," he told them. "If she's skinny."

Lynn said, "She's got to be skinny? Have fun, Amy."

"Hey, wait a minute," Amy said.

"I want to take both you guys," he said, looking uncomfortable. "This makes it tough."

"Not really tough," Lynn said. "I have to help my folks move this weekend, anyway. Take Amy."

She knew her parents were pretending to be happy about the smaller house. It was still within walking distance of school, and having her in a good school was one of the main things that had brought them in from the country. But she and Amy wouldn't be living four minutes away from each other anymore. She wasn't happy about it, but she couldn't very well lock herself in her room and refuse to pack up and move.

Amy said, "Just go by yourself, Josh. Tell us what it's like."

He stared at both of them a long time, and spread his hands. "This is the dumbest setup three people ever had."

On Saturday Amy came over early to help Lynn and her folks settle into the new place. She found Lynn in a room with awful green walls. She stared around. "What are you doing — trying to make it look exactly like the room you just left?"

"Yes," Lynn said, shoving furniture determinedly. "I liked it the way it was."

Amy smiled. "Me too. I was — you know — afraid it would be different here. Without a place for me anymore." She walked around the room, picking up things of her own that had made the move from the other house. "Hey, here's my poster I'd forgotten about. Want to hang it up?"

Lynn's mother brought in a carton of linens. She gave Lynn a glance that said, "Reassure her." Lynn said, "Sure. It'll always be your room, too, silly. Your house." Her mom smiled.

They got the bed up, and helped put the kitchen and bath in working order. Amy slept over. In the dark she said, "I wish Josh was as lucky as I am. To have a place."

"He's got a place," Lynn reminded her. "It's just that nobody's ever there." Both of Josh's parents worked nights. About the only times he saw them was when they passed each other as he came home from school and they started to work.

"But don't you think he's lonely?" Amy asked.

"I think he gladly goes home to that empty house and recuperates from knowing us," Lynn said. They giggled.

Sunday, while they were unpacking books, Amy suddenly said, "Well, was he noble yesterday? Did he refuse to go up because we all couldn't go — or was he human?"

Lynn surprised herself by answering, "What difference does it make? I wish he wasn't getting to be so special to us."

"Why?" Amy asked.

Lynn tore open a carton of books instead of answering.

Amy said, "Three people being friends IS pretty special. We can't help it — it's rare. Besides, he needs us. Remember when you and I got to be friends, how good it was to have somebody?" She studied Lynn's face curiously. "You don't think he might begin to like one of us better than the other, do you?"

Lynn felt her face go hot. "Why would I think that?"

"That's what I mean," Amy said. "Why would you? He knows we're best friends and he has to take us as a set. Tweedledum and Tweedledee."

"The Tweedledumbest setup three people ever had?" Lynn asked. Amy smiled, looking relieved, and caught a ride home as Lynn's dad went back to the old house for one final load.

The next morning at school they stopped Josh in the hall. "Well, what's soaring like?"

"Thrill of a lifetime!" he said excitedly.

They glanced at each other. "Human," Lynn said.

Josh said, "We did this tight spiral, and caught a thermal that shot us straight up. Straight up! I was telling Amy last night — "

He stopped, looking uncertain. Amy said quickly, "He called. He was describing what it was like. He didn't have your number yet."

"Oh," Lynn said. "Sure. That's right." She blinked rapidly, trying to focus her thoughts. It was true — he didn't know her new number. But couldn't he have waited? She fixed a smile on her face and listened as Josh described the wind-sounds and tilting white wings. Amy was listening intently. Couldn't you have said, "Wait and tell us both tomorrow?" Lynn asked her in her mind.

How tacky can I get? she wondered. After all, I had to help move, so I couldn't go. But Amy gave up her thrill-of-a-lifetime ride without having to. She deserved a preview.

She pushed the incident away, feeling small and picky. But a few days later her mother said, "What's making you so hard to live with, doll?"

"I hate new things!" she answered. "I hate starting over. I want things to stay the same."

Her mother said, "Let's go buy some paint and get rid of those pea-soup walls. You'll feel better."

Amy and Josh came the next afternoon to help her paint. By the time the pale-pink room was finished, night had come and a hard spring rain was beating at the windows. They washed the brushes and rollers in the kitchen sink, and scrubbed their hands.

"Alas, what dread disease is this?" Josh asked, dabbing at the paint-measles on Lynn's face with a cup towel.

She tried to think of something Shakespearean and clever to answer, but couldn't, and glanced at Amy for help.

"Gadzooks," Amy exclaimed, "we do be doomed — by the pink plague!"

Their hammy gestures reminded Lynn of something. "Oh, listen — Miss Steiner asked me if we'd like to do a skit for the Final Follies in May."

"And you said?" they prompted her.

"I said I'd ask you."

"Just the three of us?" Amy groaned. "That's going to take weeks, Lynnie. Thinking it up. Practicing."

"But you knew we would," Josh said, grinning. "How much time do we have and what kind of skit does she want?"

Lynn grinned back in relief. "I'll ask. She made a few suggestions that we can sort of build around. And we can make costumes here, if we need to. Daddy fixed my mom's sewing machine after we killed it doing the Three Blind Mice."

Suddenly the lights flickered and went out. Amy squealed. They fell silent. Josh said, "Power's off," and pulled them close, one in each arm. "I'll keep you safe."

Amy giggled and said, "I don't know about this. You probably attract lightning the way you attract girls."

Thunder crashed above them. Lynn gave a start, glad that Josh's protecting arm tightened around her waist.

"Mice, I want you to know something," he said in a soft rush. "You two are the best friends I ever had. Since I've known you — this is the happiest I've ever been in my life. So I just wanted to let you know, and say thank you — and it's easier in the dark."

Lynn felt the warm surge of her own happiness spread through her.

"Easier in the dark to let you know it's mutual," Amy answered.

A glow appeared in the hall. Lynn's mother aimed a flashlight at them. "There you are — I was worried." She went on past, and the glow disappeared, but not before it had swept across Josh's and Amy's faces tilted together in a kiss.

Lynn's dad called, "I think I better take you kids home now — the storm's nearly over."

Lynn felt Josh's hand slide up and give her shoulder a gentle squeeze, before it dropped away.

For a second she was afraid to move. Wasn't he going to kiss her, too? To seal a sweet special moment? Or had the flashlight and the necessity of leaving distracted him?

61

Her heart began to pound. Emotions fell over each other in the darkness of her head. She couldn't stand there, waiting, if it wasn't going to happen. She took a step out of his reach, glad that their faces were gray blurs.

Her dad came in, feeling his way. "Okay, gang, let's run for the car." Amy and Josh started out. Her dad turned around. "Babe, aren't you coming along for the ride?"

"No," she said almost inaudibly.

I'm sorry, Miss Flannery. You know I always try for upbeat endings. But what can I do with this?

FOR MR. AND MRS. BRIAN MCGEE

Dear Mom and Dad,

It seems like a long time. I hope you're okay.

I know you're doing everything you can. Don't give up. I'm still here.

It will all come together. They'll find that man. Or he'll brag to somebody. Or try to get money out of you.

Then they'll make him say where he's put me. And you'll come.

I think about it. I jerked awake a few minutes ago, certain that I'd heard your voices.

Why would he pick me? I turn it around and around in my mind. Was it just a spaced-out whim of his, and I happened to be there? Did he think he could get a big ransom out of you? Boy, did I look that rich in my discount-store raincoat?

Maybe he thought he was getting April.

Doesn't that seem to be a reasonable explanation? Think about it — her dad being a lawyer could be the key to it all. A grudge thing. This guy fresh out of prison where Mr. Beckner put him. Now Beckner's kid is going to pay for those lost years, see? It happens like that all the time in old movies.

No point in telling April, though. She might think I was wishing this on her. You've probably noticed already that she and I are having troubles. It's personal. Maybe I can talk about it when I don't feel so emotional. Anyway, it's queer to think about my being here and her safe at home, when maybe it was supposed to have been the other way around.

If her dad's getting ransom notes, that's why.

I get confused sometimes. My mind blocks off big chunks of time. It's like bumping into furniture that's been rearranged — I keep remembering the way April and I were, instead of that afternoon she came to our house and ran off with her arms full of stuff.

Sometimes I imagine how different it would have been if he had taken us BOTH — how we would have talked and cried, and then pulled ourselves together and explored the ceiling, one climbing up on the other's shoulders or something. We'd find some kind of vent, and wham the typewriter against it until it broke and we could crawl out of here. Then we'd write a play about our adventures. A script — we've always said we'd do a script — and it would be a prize-winning movie and April could play herself and I could be Technical Adviser or whatever it's called.

Anyway, having her would have helped. Well, maybe not, the way things are. I was forgetting again. But this is hard to do, alone. You were always saying I ought to have other friends, and not do everything with April and be so dependent on her. I see what you mean, but a person needs to have a special other person to be with. Talking. Planning. Laughing at each other's jokes. You two have each other.

We were trying to open up. Zack was a good start — you said so yourselves. The trouble is, there was only one of him and two of us.

I wonder if the man who brought me here made a choice — eenie, meenie, minie, mo — in that second when he was holding April and me by the arms. Was there something that made him choose me?

I wonder if April could have managed this. By herself. If he had picked her.

I wonder if I can.

Find me, please. This is hard to take.

Love,
Jackie

TTM

I cried a long time. Don't know what set me off, but I cried until I was worn out and slept. I don't know how long. The slit is dark.

Part of me wants to sleep a lot. It's a way to let the time go by without feeling the floor or smelling the stink or thinking about my folks and home and life going on out there. Another part of me is afraid someone will call my name, or tap on the door, testing, and I won't hear it.

When I woke up I couldn't get oriented. Very shaky. Headache. Probably nothing a good pizza and a walk in the sunshine couldn't cure.

Stiff upper lip, Jackie — whiny girls don't deserve

Forgot what I was saying.

I'll remember it. Just have heavy things on my mind.

Got to keep pounding out words words words, or my

brain is going to start sneaking questions into the empty spaces.

WHAT I WILL DO FIRST

Take bath. Wash hair. Brush moss off teeth.

Eat whole watermelon.

Look at the sky twenty-four hours.

Sit on warm ground, touch grass.

Run in wind. Sing. See what time it is.

Flush toilet.

Read paper. Listen to music.

Forget this happened.

But it happened. I've been fooling myself. I can't do that anymore. This is serious. I'm in a place nobody comes to. An old abandoned farm. Or storage area. Maybe broken windows, boarded up, and signs that say, "Warning, No Trespassing, Condemned." A high fence around the whole place, with only one little unlocked gate, or hole to sneak through, and he's the only one who knows about it.

Or maybe he lives in this place. Maybe it's his home. And every day he walks over to the cellar door and picks up my letters. And smiles. And crumples them up.

What do you want with me, damn you? You know who I mean. Coward. No-face geek. Are you crazy? Did some Voice tell you to grab a girl off the street and bury her alive?

I don't know what to do. Isn't anybody coming? Ever?

TO THE SHICKLEY HEIGHTS POLICE

I started to write you a businesslike letter. I can't. This is ridiculous.

What's holding things up out there? What's the foul-up? Isn't anybody looking for me? Or are you telling my folks not to worry — I'm probably just a runaway? Typical mixed-up teenager, driving off with some guy in his van because I had a fight with a boy friend — or I'm not happy at home — or I'm a misfit at school — or I'm not great-looking or something?

You're not going to make them believe that. Listen to them. I mean really listen! They know me better than you do.

Yes, I had a personal problem with two friends, but it doesn't have any connection with this.

Get the facts from April Beckner. Let her tell you how the guy pushed her down and shoved me into the van and drove off. She IS telling you that, isn't she? You're not putting it into her head that this is some sick revenge I thought up — that I got this geek to whisk me away to scare her into a guilt attack, are you?

Honestly, the one and only time I really told April a lie was once when I pretended I sprained my wrist at school so I could go home and finish a report that was due. Big deal, right? Even then I felt so tacky when she came over to see how I was, lugging homemade cupcakes, that I decided right then that I'd rather tell her the truth. And I have.

And I'm telling you the truth, too. This is serious. I wouldn't do a crazy, dangerous thing like this, even to pay her back for what she did.

But where are you? Aren't you even trying?

If I sound peculiar, it's probably this new starvation diet I'm trying out. It's nothing like the great jailhouse food your inmates get. This stuff puts hammers in your head. I will mail this letter, anyway. Any law says I can't?

Get on the ball, out there.

> Jackie McGee
> the girl who disappeared

TTM

I don't think that last letter was exactly Respectful of Authority. I probably wouldn't have mailed it if I had stopped to think. I don't know. My moods swing back and forth like Tarzan on a vine. It's frustrating not to be able to look back over what I've said. But anyway, it's mailed. Even with no light coming from the slit, I just kept pushing the paper around up there till I felt it slide through.

No, I'm glad I sent it. What kind of trusting idiot do they think I am, sitting here patiently while they tell my folks I'll very likely show up safe and sound when I've thought things over!

Okay, I AM a certain kind of trusting idiot. I got taken. Literally. I was tricked. Gullible is the word for me, isn't it, Miss Flannery?

I've been kidnapped. I've got to face that word. Somebody kidnapped me and put me here. I don't know why. There has to be a reason, an explanation, but I don't know it. So to me it's senseless. That scares me. I don't like being someone's victim. I don't want to be a bug that gets stepped on and nobody even notices. Being helpless is an awful thing.

Sometimes I think words are all I have. I get to pick and choose and line them up in rows. If you can feel your pulse you're still alive, right? So I keep the pulse going. Clip-clop, clip-clop. The sound of me.

I'm trying to think what my best memories are. It's hard to know where to start. So many things. Moonrises. Fireworks. Sleep-overs, giggling all night. Birthdays. Writing a really honest poem. I've had good times.

BEST MEMORIES

It was the Christmas before I was six and we could make jokes because they knew that I knew by then, and my dad said, "Well, look at this — old Santa had to put the package in through the window, here behind the couch, because he couldn't squeeze down that eight-inch stovepipe." And I opened the box and there was a little, furry puppy-head. They said, "What do you want to call him?" And out of somewhere I said, "Gillenwater Goodboy," and they gulped and said, "That's a fine big name." And he liked it so much he threw up.

My first day at Dupree, April came up and gave me a long stare. She said, "Did you notice we're wearing sweaters alike? Even the same little dribble on the front. What's yours?" And I said, grabbing at the most foreign thing I could think of, "Anchovy juice." Her mouth dropped open, and she said, "You're kidding. My dribble is anchovy juice, too." And she led me off to show me Dupree. We were like two magnets clicking together. We didn't tell each other for a year that neither of us had ever tasted anchovies.

Haply I think on thee, April. As I alone beweep my outcast state. You see? I can talk Shakespeare, too.

I won't forget how you took me for a friend and nearly became the other half of me. I won't forget how together you and Zack made my life complete from A to Z.

But that was then.

If I could just read. I pretend I'm holding books. I read them in Braille. I find out all about the Louisiana Purchase. I feel the pictures. No — would there be pictures? Maps. The Oregon Trail goes squiggling off into the distance.

Okay, it's better now. Had to double-bag part of the poop pile to stop a leak. Gruesome. But we want to keep the place tidy, right? Hey, Mom, get me out of here and I promise to clean the bathroom three times a day. Scrub the tub, down through the porcelain to cast iron. Scrub the toothpaste. Scrub the toilet paper.

It's strange that in the dark I can shift beautiful designs behind my eyelids like a kaleidoscope. I try to keep my mind filled with pictures. I play games, like remembering my room, foot by foot. The color it gets, as the sun rises and lights the sky and finally eases in at the window.

The books, the old faded ones. I pick names of colors for them — plum and pewter and mauve and ashes-of-roses and terra cotta. Then the new ones still in their jackets, shiny and eye-catching. The curtains moving, leaf-shadows running up and down. The ceiling reflecting the pink in the walls, and the dusty little spiderwebs swaying in some mysterious breeze.

The loneliness hurts like a bruise.

I wonder what I look like. My hair feels all tangled and different. I never realized until I was in here that I always sort of peeped into the mirror every morning to say hi, and make sure I was okay.

Am I the same? If the hair has changed, maybe the rest of me has, too.

I try so hard not to let go.

I see this special detective. The one in the crime show who never gives up. Keeps sifting through the bits for clues no one has noticed yet. He tells my folks, "She's out there somewhere, depending on us. We're going to find her." I almost cry.

I have times when I'm afraid to look up for fear I'll see that door being lifted slowly, and No-Face looking down. But quick as a flash I make it the detective's face. Or my dad's. Or even Zack's. Is that you down there, Jackie? Yes! It's me.

Sometimes I re-create home. I see my mom getting ready in the morning. Always running so late that her robe flies out behind her, getting caught in all the doors. And the little notes from her second-graders that she sticks on the bathroom mirror to keep her spirits up. I loved the Christmas one that said, "I hope you have a hart-worming hollyday."

And Daddy's toenails shooting off in all directions when he cuts them. I would love to step on a toenail clipping. I would love to hear him yell when Mom squirts hand lotion on his hands before he can stop her. I can see his chapped hands. Grease lines like the roads on maps. I see him letting her rub pink perfumed stuff around the black edges of his nails and the scrapes and cuts, and I can tell by their faces they're thinking getting to bed and for a while in the dark no second-graders, no fried transmissions, just love.

I want my detective to come. Tough guy. Pussycat inside. He glances down in here at me. "Kid, I've lost a hell of a lot of sleep over you. Climb out of that hole and get yourself home where you belong."

So, where is he?

I know it's childish.

So, okay. But if you ask me, all of us are part children and part grown-up. Some things we're mature about, some things reduce up to baby-brains. Like, my dad would die if he thought he has eaten pineapple. And once my mom cried when one of her second-graders lied to his parents and said she hit him. Broke her heart.

I must have been a pain to my folks, taking my good sweet time to grow up. To partly grow up.

I feel so low. Really down.

I try not to let it get a grip on me, but

Butbutbut what?

I make up happy things behind my eyelids. People walking. The table set. Then I open my eyes.

Those blind fish that live in rivers down inside caves — I wonder if they have some ancient memory of what's out there in the sun. Do pictures and patterns and lights play inside their heads, trying to remind them?

My dad said when I was little and had walked a long way, he used to ask me, did I want to walk like a big girl, or be carried like a baby?

Carried now, Daddy.

DEAR MISS FLANNERY,

I know you said a short story ought to be all of a piece. I've been thinking about my characters. Maybe this will have to be a novel, with time passing and people growing, like real life. Might as well make it long. Not a lot of things going on in here to take up my time.

Most people read to escape, don't they? I write.

Can I tell you something? You gave me such a hard time, pounding grammar into me last year, that I sort of went along with April and Zack and gave you a hard time. Like the project we did on "I Am the Cheese," dressed in our old mice costumes. We must have added some gray hairs to your collection.

Anyway, I just want to say I feel different now. I see reasons behind a lot of the things you taught us. The connections are coming. So I just wanted to thank you for believing I was worth struggling with.

A STORY
(second part)

It seemed appropriate that they first went to their special place almost exactly a year after Amy and Lynn first met Josh, on the same kind of gray winter day, too, when spring seemed far away. By that time they had the feeling that they had known each other all their lives and there were no surprises left.

Lynn actually discovered the spot. She was in the car with her mom and dad when they started arguing and she said, "Just let me get out and walk around, okay? And when you're ready, pick me up." So they let her out and she watched the car circle the lake to the far side and disappear beyond the closed-up cottages and rickety boathouses. Gradually her shivers stopped and she walked past the molting cattails and tattered red sumac into a thicket. Unexpectedly, at its center, she found herself standing in an open hollow full of light, another little world.

She took Amy and Josh out to see it the next weekend. Or, rather, Josh took them. He worked part-time for Classy Grass, mowing lawns in summer and doing yardwork year-round, and the two guys he worked for were pretty casual about letting him borrow the truck.

They drove up as close as they could on the little dirt road. Lynn jumped out, excited about her find, but Josh and Amy peered up at the heavy cold clouds and took their time. They were at a completely deserted end of the lake. Far in the distance a train whistle blew.

"What are we supposed to do out here?" Amy asked, shivering by the chrome-colored water. "This had better be good, Lynnie."

"At least she didn't say bring swimsuits," Josh murmured.

"Come and see what's back here," Lynn said, and crashed off through the thicket. They shrugged and followed. The trees got larger. Weeds and brush crackled as they pushed through them. Up ahead Lynn stopped and waited.

"What's the matter?" Amy asked.

Lynn beckoned. They drew up on either side of her at the edge of the little hollow. It had been the clearing for a farmhouse once — an old chimney had crumbled to rubble in the grass.

"Hey, nice," Josh said softly. "A little lost place."

Lynn flushed with pleasure at his reaction. She nodded.

Josh crunched through the weeds to a spot with a sagging fence around it. "What's this?"

Lynn went to his side. "Somebody's garden." She went inside at an old broken gate. "See, these are dried asparagus stalks. And old berry bushes. Still coming back every year, even with nobody to care for them."

Impulsively she stooped and pulled weeds away from the plants.

Amy edged closer, catching her jacket on the brambles. "How can you tell? I thought berries came from the frozen-food section of the supermarket."

"We had a garden once," Lynn said.

Amy asked, "Will asparagus spears really come up here in the spring?"

"They'll try," Lynn said. "They'd do a lot better if we could find some manure to put around them."

"Manure?" Amy made a long face. "Don't tell me that — I love asparagus. DID love it. No wonder it makes your pee smell funny."

"Would you rather eat a plant that likes chewed-up grass spread around it — or a dead cow?" Lynn asked.

Josh said, "I can get some manure. We can bring a load out in the truck."

"Gross," Amy moaned. Josh and Lynn grinned at each other.

"Try to git ahold of yorself, gal," he said. "Them that don't shovel shit don't git to come back next spring for the reward."

Amy folded her arms firmly. "You guys are actually suggesting that we could come back to this wilderness area and produce produce?"

Josh said, "Give that little lady a bushel of zucchini!"

"We could bring seeds," Lynn said in a burst of excitement. Her eyes were shiny. "And plant our very own tomatoes and beans and sweet corn—"

"And carry water from the lake when it didn't rain," Josh added, giving the gate a tug to straighten it.

"AND fight bugs and weeds and whatever comes out of the woods to eat veggies," Amy said. "Think mosquitoes, you dreamers."

Lynn walked slowly to a tree at the edge of the hollow, and studied its broken spreading limbs. "We'd need to prune the apple tree."

Amy stared at it. "That thing will have apples?" She slowly smiled, enchanted. "You mean I could pick a real apple?"

"Just like Snow White," Lynn laughed.

"I think you mean Eve," Josh said.

Amy hit him on the nose with a weed. "Okay, you two. You win. Let's go for the garden."

So they did. Josh borrowed rakes and hoes and pruners from his bosses. He brought a reeking load of manure from a turkey farm. They cleaned up the old plot. By the time Josh's requests to use the truck after hours began to be turned down, they learned they could catch a bus out to the lake, mornings, and back in before night. On a bright April day they planted the first

Broke off, Miss Flannery. Thought I heard something. A little TICK TICK TICK.

All I could think was, I'm rescued!

My throat locked up. I couldn't breathe, or even move. I just waited for another sound, louder, closer. But there wasn't anything else. I yelled. I hit the door, screaming that I was in here. But by then I knew it had been something here inside that had made that tiny noise.

Gradually I reached out along the walls and floor with my shoe in my hand, scared I might come across something soft and squirmy — a mouse or even a snake. I don't know how old this place is. How long it's been empty. Or what might have come up through that little drain in the floor, or dropped down from a crack in that ceiling I can't see or touch.

Anyway, there's nothing but silence now. Not even a plastic bread wrapper crinkling as something inside molds and collapses. Could it have been an insect hatching or whatever they do? Do I have a roommate? Little eyes looking at me in the dark? Little feelers checking out the coffeecake?

I wanted it to be somebody. So bad.

The story flew out of my head. I don't know where I stopped.

I have to stay calm about this. It was just a tiny sound. But someday it's going to be the clang of that door opening and stopping me right in mid-sentence. It is!

I'm not prepared for you, No-Face. I don't know what I'll do if it's ever you again. Will you be coming to let me out? Bringing me more food? Or something else? Do I try to rush past you up those steps, and run? Do I try to be reasonable? What if you're sick and can't reason? Will I have to protect myself? What if I managed to cut your eyes with my lipstick top, and then discovered you were some addled little guy they'd kicked out of a mental institution too soon?

We've all watched so much TV we take it for granted I'm going to get raped and murdered and dismembered and all sorts of good wholesome prime-time stuff. Why don't we ever hear about some trashed-out guy who kidnaps somebody, then comes and lets her out, apologizing, and drives off to Alaska to grow cabbages?

It's not news anymore that we have dark places in us and that terrible things come out sometimes. But what we really want and love is the light, isn't it? Everybody.

The sunny side of this is that you HAVEN'T come back, No-Face. I keep telling myself you won't. If you had rape on your mind I'd have known about it that night. I think it's something else. Just a job, for money, maybe. Or some compulsion you're in the grip of. And now you've gone underground. You're hiding. They'll have to force you out.

They will. Believe me — they will!

And when you're caught, I want to watch the law chew you up into little pieces.

It's strange. I have to face the fact that every hour I spend in here is changing me. I guess the scariest change is that I'm actually accepting the idea that unexplainable things like this can fall out of the sky on people, without warning.

I doubt that I'll ever feel safe again in small dark places. Closets. Elevators. I imagine I'll climb a lot of stairs.

I guess thinking a lot about revenge would make my life different.

One thing's already different — I'll never be able to take the ordinary day-by-day things for granted anymore. Food. Water. Control. Light. Freedom. Air to breathe.

It seems odd, but when I begin to write, folding the raincoat to sit on, getting the paper into the typewriter — by the time I'm ready, all the sweating and panic and horror is disappearing like some kind of bus that knocked me down and sped away. I sit watching it, hurting, but so glad to be alive that I brush myself off, babbling, "Hey, I'm fine, I'm okay," so nobody will know how terrifying it really was. Even me.

When I fall into really black depression, I try to build words into rickety little steps I can climb back up on. It helps me pretend I'm in control. I'm not in control. I wake up with my face on the floor. I live in my own personal sewage tank, poking plastic wrappers to be sure I'm choosing stale pumpernickel and not solid waste. But I pretend.

My mind keeps trying to make this into a documentary. I interview people out there on the other side of the door.

Question: Why am I here, No-Face? For some kind of punishment? Did you need to hide me for some reason? To give yourself time for something? It doesn't make sense.

Answer: Sounds like you're scraping the bottom of the barrel for questions.

Q: Why are you out there? Are you going to open the door, or not?

A: Which would you rather?

Q: Open it! Wait. I don't know. Right now all I want is to keep you in suspension. Stopped. Sitting in your van. Or a cheap room, watching TV, reading what the papers are saying. Sweating a lot, like in the movies.

A: It's not real sweat. They spray it on, just before they shoot the scene.

Q: You're trying to confuse me. Make me think scary things. You can stop — I admit to being scared out of my skull. You don't play by the rules.

A: I just don't play by your rules, April.

Q: I'm not April! I'm Jackie McGee. I'm April's friend. I mean — not really, anymore.

A: Yeah? I'm Thurmond Smith. Or Ronnie Peeples. Or — I don't know anymore. I have different names, too.

Q: I've got names for you. Sadistic lump of slime. Coldblooded, treacherous, unnatural —

A: Hey, call me Ronnie. And calm down. You just don't like being at the mercy of somebody who does senseless things, April.

Q: Stop saying "April"! I need answers from you. Are you going to let me out? Are you going to hurt me? What's the reason for all this? IS there a reason?

A: There's always a reason.

Q: Then what's yours? Are you insane? Was this all a mistake? Are you in jail and can't come back? Or were you just so stoned you dropped me in here and FORGOT about me?

A: Not so stoned or crazy that I couldn't leave you food and water, if you noticed. You want to know why I left you food and water?

Q: No.

A: Because the stale donuts used to run out at our house, too, when I was young. And sometimes the water got turned off when the old lady didn't pay the bill. So I went to the trouble, okay?

Q: I'm not listening.

A: Suit yourself.

Q: You could be dead.

A: So could you, hon.

Q: Stop that. Are you dead?

A: Jeez, I never noticed.

Q: You are. You can't tell anybody where I am.

A: How could I be dead? I'm talking to you. Okay. Maybe a little dead. Maybe the part that decides right from wrong is a little bit dead.

Q: Please open the door and let me out, No-Face. Thurmond. Ronnie. I'll do anything. I'm begging. I'll swear I never saw you before. I'll never tell anybody what happened.

A: You wouldn't need to worry about telling anybody anything. If I came.

Q: What do you mean? Stop. This documentary is over. The end. Stop talking.

A: Whatever you say, hon.

THE STORY
(continued)

So the garden was planted, but for the next month it took second place. The skit for the Final Follies had to be ready by the middle of May.

It was fun, but a lot of work. They batted ideas back and forth until their brains rattled. They actually wrote songs, and Miss Steiner made them sing and hum until she worked out piano arrangements. They gathered costumes and made the main prop they needed, from plywood and canvas — a pretend dumpster full of trash.

A bag lady and an old wino were going to find the dumpster and pull discarded clothes and articles out of it. Each of them would occasionally disappear behind it and come out dressed as someone richer, younger, more successful. Finally they would end up as students, making outrageous comments on all the current situations at school. Amy and Josh kept saying, "Lynnie, make it three people, poking through the trash." But Lynn said, "It would look too busy. I want to be the stagehand hidden behind the dumpster, helping you with costume changes and handing you props."

The night finally came. The auditorium filled up with parents and kids. The three of them were waiting backstage to go on next when Amy in her bag-lady clothes and tangled wig suddenly screamed, "My hat — my crazy-hat — it's still in the locker!"

She hoisted her skirt and headed for the door. Lynn stopped her, ordering, "Go back — you can't run in those clodhopper shoes. I'll get it."

She darted out into the hall. The lockers were in a wing on the other side of the building. She cut through the dim empty library, and clattered down a flight of metal stairs. The wing was dark. She groped along the wall for a light switch, found it, and ran to the locker. Her nervous fingers fumbled over the combination lock. Four-letter words escaped on her breath. Why hadn't they noticed sooner? They had to have the hat; it was part of the plot, and they had worked to make it perfectly horrible and hilarious.

The lock clicked. She grabbed the sack with the hat in it and ran again, slapping the light off as she passed. Halfway up the stairs she tripped and lunged forward. Her knees hit the metal edge of a step and grated across the rough surface beyond it. She grabbed for the railing, missed, slid down three steps, and finally caught herself. "Damn!" she yelled, hunting the sack. She started up the stairs more slowly, shaken and dazed. At the top she began to run again.

She could hear applause as she neared the auditorium. The gymnasts who came before their skit had finished. She rushed backstage, past people bringing off mats. Miss Steiner said, "Good lord, Jackie!" and tackled her as she passed.

"I've got to get onstage, behind the dumpster," she gasped. She could see it, out there. Amy and Josh were posed in their places, staring tautly at the closed curtain.

"Not with those knees," Miss Steiner said. She yanked the sack from Lynn's fingers and sent it slithering out across the stage. Josh kicked it behind the dumpster and leaped back into his pose.

"Oh, please — they need me!" Lynn begged, lunging inside Miss Steiner's arm. But the curtain glided open.

Miss Steiner beckoned another teacher over. "Some gauze and tape," she whispered. On stage, Amy and Josh exchanged their first lines. A ripple of laughter came from the audience. She turned back to Lynn. "You will lie down over there. Don't move until I come back." She hurried to the piano just offstage, strained forward to catch the cue, and began to pound out the first song.

Lynn felt the teacher press her down on the couch. "But I'm okay, and they can't manage without me!" she protested. The ache in her throat surprised her more than the blood on her knees. "They'll think I let them down."

The teacher said, "Be still. We don't need gauze here — we need Hamburger Helper."

Lynn closed her eyelids over her tears and lay back. She let herself be bandaged and questioned. She listened to the songs and the laughter, and at last the roar of applause as the skit ended. She watched Amy and Josh bounce offstage into the wings, sweaty and triumphant. She saw Miss Steiner motion to them to take a bow. For an instant they seemed to hesitate, glancing through the crowd and clutter. "I tried!" she almost yelled. But they turned, catching hands, and walked back into the glare of lights and a new wave of applause.

They had managed it without her.

She bit her lip, trying to feel her own reward and success through them.

When they finally found her and had heard what happened, she asked how they had done it. Amy said, "We just changed costumes as fast as we could without you — sometimes we came out from behind the dumpster still getting into things. Maybe that made it even funnier."

Josh said, "They loved it, Lynnie. It was worth all the work, wasn't it?"

Miss Steiner, satisfied that Lynn was not going to be a paraplegic or sue the school, let her get up and hobble around, helping to gather up the props and costumes. Lynn's folks came backstage. Her dad said they were great, and took their boxes to the car. Her mother said, "I loved that part at the end where you broke into the dance." She twirled around, singing in her unsteady voice, "YOU have what YOU have to give — no one's a zero — YOU have your OWN life to live — so be a hero!" She almost had the tune right. She straightened Lynn's droopy hair. "Well, doll, for years you and Amy have said you're Broadway-bound. Now I believe it."

They all laughed. Lynn's dad came back in. "There's still room in the car for five."

Amy said, "My dad's coming by after his meeting. I think it's sort of to make up for not being here to see us. So I'll wait for him."

Josh said, "I guess I ought to stay, too, and get her home, in case he happens not to show up." He looked at Lynn. "Give those knees a rest, mouse."

Lynn limped out behind her folks. At the door she turned around. "We did it," she said.

Their faces, still in makeup, smiled at her, dark-eyed and different. "It's only the beginning!" Amy called back.

DEAR MOM AND DAD,

I'm mailing you the latest installment of that award-winning sitcom called Jackie's Joint. This week, Jackie, a scatterbrained teenager, struggles to write a breathtaking adventure story for her favorite English teacher. She is accidentally carried off by a bumbling kidnapper, but keeps scribbling furiously, not only during her captivity, but also during her dramatic rescue and a riotous welcome-home party. When she turns in her story, the teacher says, "Rather inflated and melodramatic, Jackie. You can do better."

Like it? I think it's terrific.

I love you. I miss you. I don't know what to say.

I feel better than I have in — what do you call them out there? — days. Things are going fine here. I know things are going fine out there, too, and it's only a matter of time.

I'm just sad that you've had to worry about me, and think the worst, and all that. I know how you feel. When I was little, that was always the most terrible fear I had. That you'd go away, or get divorced, or something would happen to you and I wouldn't have you. I just couldn't bear the idea.

When it happened to April, and her mother actually took off, I couldn't bear it for her, either.

I know you've always said the time would come when other people and my career and things would be more important in my life than you. I hope it works the other way around, too, and I'm just there in your lives, nice but not as important as your jobs and feelings for each other and plans for the future and all that. So this thing, this separation, will be something you can handle. I hope you haven't let me become so important that you've built your lives around me. Knocking yourselves out to give me things you thought I needed. Changing yourselves to fit me. Don't do that.

Sometimes I wish we could go back to our first house out in the country. Do you think Gillie is still alive — would he remember us if we took him back? I know we can't go back. But I think about it.

I pretend sometimes that this is an elevator and that I can make believe it's stopping and letting me out at any place I want it to. I can step off at any level I want.

The penthouse, please. I could do with some sky.

I could do with a bath, too. Didn't I read about somebody who said he was so dirty he was beginning to have geological significance?

You're going to be so glad to get me back you'll let me soak for two hours and never yell, "Next!" through the bathroom door. You're going to stay at home from work a whole day and sit looking at me and grinning. I love you. Did I say that already? I love you so much.

Your kid,
Jackie

DEAR GILLENWATER GOODBOY,

My dear wiggly waggly warm friend. Dear hand-licker companion. Dear cold nose in the night, checking to see if I was still there and all right.

Did you realize that we were in a race those first years? First you were the puppy, and I could lug you around, then suddenly you were strong enough and big enough to knock me down and make me cry. Then I grew, too, and by the time I was seven we were matched, and after that you stayed your final size, so small you had to jump up on people to be petted. And I went on.

But you learned things so much faster than I did, and understood so many things that I'm still struggling with. Doesn't that seem strange?

I think about you, Gillie. I dreamed about you again. Your bowl was empty and I was hunting something for it. You were a puppy, but I was like I am now. You followed me along, trustfully, with that smile of yours. You really could smile, you know. Like Buster Brown's dog.

I don't know why I'm telling you this. You're an old fellow now, if you're still alive. An old stiff dog with cloudy eyes. I hope you've been happy, and Donna and David from down the road have been good to you and loved you. So much that you don't remember anymore that we gave you away and left.

I guess I hope you've forgotten me.

Be a good dog.

Your friend 4 ever,
Jackie

THE STORY

Anyway, the garden grew into an Eden. They had planted twice as much as they needed. They gave away radishes and lettuce on the bus. Lynn's dad was so impressed he asked if he could drive by and see it. He walked between the rows, silent, his eyes touching everything.

Before he left, he told her how she could cut the branches of a fallen tree into poles, and set them up crisscrossed over the string-bean rows to give the vines something to twine on.

Now that school was out, Lynn had time to make the long trip out on her bike while Amy was baby-sitting or stuck in one of the boring enrichment classes Mr. Beckner was always signing her up for, and Josh was busy at Classy Grass. She made the beanpole corridor with her dad's hatchet, whacking away all one day.

Before the big leaves covered them and turned them into a long skinny green tent, the crossed poles reminded her of pictures she'd seen of those military weddings where the bride and groom passed under a row of raised sabers.

She liked surprising Amy and Josh with something new every time they came out. Three little seats of old unearthed bricks, padded with grass. A bottle of insect repellent stashed handy in a hollow tree. Little dried gourds to drink from.

On the Fourth of July they carried out a big bowl, and salad dressing and plates and forks and bits of cheese and ham. They made a gigantic salad and ate it by the lake, letting the water lap over their hot feet. Later, as they dozed at the edge of their hollow while faraway firecrackers popped on the opposite shore, Josh said, "How about we live here forever?"

Lynn sat up, and checked Amy, who, without opening her eyes, asked, "Can we put in a shopping mall?"

"Nope. Just us," Josh said.

Lynn took a deep luxurious breath. She had been thinking how beautiful it was to be lying there, the three of them, complete and at peace.

He said, "Don't you ever just want to screw everything — school — everybody — and just take off? Just do what YOU want to do, for a change?"

She shrugged, not sure how to answer. She was doing what she wanted to do.

Josh turned to her in the dappled shade of the apple tree. "But maybe that's not such a great idea, with you planning to write all that award-winning stuff, and Amy planning to be the star of whatever all you can be a star of."

Lynn smiled at him. "Do you suppose they'd read my plays if I sent them in written on pieces of bark?"

"Wow, the postage," Amy mumbled, half asleep. "Wouldn't it be simpler if Josh just lived with us in New York?"

Josh stared at the sky with his eagle-sharp eyes. "I don't know. I really believe you two are going to do big wild things like that. You are. I wouldn't ruin it for you."

His voice was so wistful Lynn wanted to take his hands. She said, "Hey, you're going to do great things, too. Whatever you're hoping for." She broke into the ridiculous song from their skit. "YOU have what YOU have to give."

"Be a hero!" Amy sang out.

"Or a big empty goose-egg zero," he said.

"You have your own life to live," they sang to him, wavering off into laughter. He made a rueful face and laughed, too. That night of the Final Follies was something they would never forget.

"What we ought to do," Amy said, curling up again, "before we settle down to fame and fortune, is to go around the world."

They stared at each other, grinning, letting the magical idea sink in.

"How?" Lynn asked. It had been a dream she hadn't dared to put words to.

"Bicycles?" Josh suggested. "Stay in hostels? Go on one of those cheap freighters — maybe even work our way."

A shiver of joy went through Lynn. "We really could," she said in awe. "At least the United States. Buy an old car —"

"No. The world," Josh said. "The world, mouse. People do it all the time."

"Would your folks let you?"

His face closed up. "My folks might not even notice I was gone."

Lynn began to pitch dead leaves into the air. "Oh, this is crazy! Let's do it. Really do it."

Amy suddenly got to her feet and walked away.

Josh turned to Lynn, puzzled. "What's with her?"

"I think she's just sad," Lynn said. "When you said that about your folks not caring. I guess it brought back the memories."

"You mean about her mother skipping out with the Army guy?"

Lynn nodded. "Yeah. That still hurts. But the rest of it, too."

"What rest of it?"

"Well, just — not being taken. Not being chosen. Sort of left behind, like something her mother could use to dump on her dad for spite. You know?"

Josh slowly twisted a clump of grass out of the ground and studied it.

"And just the daily stuff. Having to live with her dad now, and him so busy that he never talks or listens or explains himself. Sometimes it all hits her and she gets really low."

They sat listening to the sounds of celebration across the lake.

"Did she ever tell you she had a little sister who died?" Lynn asked. "A baby sister."

Josh shook his head. "She's lucky to have you, Lynnie."

"Yeah?" She smiled at him. "My folks are good to her. I think they've helped her a lot. I'm lucky to have her, too." She pitched grass into his hair. "And we're both lucky to have you. She doesn't get those jumping-off-the-bridge days since we've known you." Josh's eyes riveted on her face so sharply that she gulped, realizing she had told him something else he hadn't known. "It was all a long time ago — I shouldn't even have mentioned it."

"Was it always just talk?" he asked, turning to look at the spot where Amy had gone out of sight. "Or did she try?"

"Just talk. Just — you know — testing the idea."

"How do you know she didn't try?"

"Because we've shared everything," she said. "Even things like that."

"What did you say to her, when she — talked about it? Jeez, I wouldn't know how to comfort anybody who didn't want to live."

"I didn't know either." She hesitated. "I just said things like, 'Forget it — that's the dumbest thing I ever heard of. There'd be a blank space in the world if you did. A blank space in me.'"

Josh studied her face for such a long time that she flushed and stood up.

She held out her hand to him. "We need to go find her. She's testing to see if we'll come. When we do, she'll say, 'Hey, I was watching that strange bird and you've scared it off.' Or something dumb like that. But she'll feel all reassured and safe again."

Josh slowly pulled up more grass. "Look, you know more about what to do when she's like this — maybe if you went by yourself—"

"No. Both of us," Lynn said. "All the reassuring she can get." She kept holding out her hand until he took it and let her pull him to his feet.

He stood close, looking down at her. "Mouse —" he said gently. He lifted her chin as if he meant to kiss her mouth.

Aching sweetness surged through her. But she backed away, clumsy with confusion. "Mice," she reminded him. "Three mice."

TTM

> The crack is back.
> Things were out of whack
> And I had lost all track
> Of time, in the black,
> Then the crack came back.

Phew. I'd better stick to skits and documentaries. But I feel better. It's day, outside.

I missed you, light. Little thread. I had stared at the spot where you faded until my eyes stung.

> Now there's nothing I lack
> Except a junk-food snack
> And a door-opening jack.

Maybe someone named Zack. No. Not anymore. I only said it because it rhymes.

Zack, I'm sort of writing you a letter.

Not really. It's more like putting down words about you.

April said you've left school. Why? I don't understand. She made it sound like you're going away, and I'm the reason. How could I be the reason?

I don't even want to think about what you're doing. I'm not ready for that. Actually I'm having trouble even knowing who you are. Is this a letter to the Zack you used to be, or the Zack I thought you were, or somebody I don't know?

I try going back to the very first day April and I barged into your life. You'd just arrived at school, and suddenly here was this matched set of goofballs hustling you off to play our little game. Was that a mystified look you had? A doubtful look? You acted as if you truly liked us both and were happy to play along. Together she and I did manage to be sort of funny and lovable, right? And it was a safe way for you not to get involved with any one person until you'd sized up everything and were ready. We were handy. Besides, you seemed as eager as we were for all the propping up you could get. Who wouldn't like getting attention in a double dose?

Then I try to bring it all forward into one of those winter nights when we'd gone past all that to something deeper. Remember the coffee table piled with junk food, and the three of us draped over the furniture, listening to music and talking about things that start with capital letters, like Life and Fate and Why-Are-We-Here?

When I get those capital-letter times now, I wish for you. Yeah, that seems strange to say, after what happened, doesn't it?

It's easy, in here, to think, "Why me?" and make everything personal and out of proportion. One of my bread wrappers springs a leak and I'm yelling curses. I forget that people live out their whole lives in boxes this size, or prisons or hospitals or slums this awful. I forget without you.

You helped me get angry, Zack. I'll never forget that. You'd listen, and when I said, "I've got to write those documentaries," you'd say, "You will." With your voice so earnest.

And then April would say something bubbleheaded and we'd all roll on the floor, breaking up.

You opened a lot of world to me, Zack. So many new ideas.

I'm amazed when I think of all the taken-for-granted beautiful magical blurred-together days I've lived. Getting out of bed, all safe and well. Clean, well-fed, loved. With twenty-five thousand more days ahead. To spend, to waste, whatever. Not even looking around. Probably bitching a blue streak. I can't believe it.

I guess they've told you what's happened to me. It's so strange, not to know how you're reacting. Where you are. Anything. Or how April feels. The three of us were so close — you'd think I'd be able to know, somehow, wouldn't you?

I wish what is happening to me could be a joke. A big hoax with a twist at the end so it will all be explained and make sense. That would be the easy way.

But right now I can't believe that's how life works. I don't think it has to explain itself or come up with a trick ending.

So I'm just here. Trying to hold out. Trying to outlast something or somebody I don't understand. The same way everyone else is trying to get past what's happened to them, I guess. Not even expecting answers.

TTM

I'm still shaking. I woke up, absolutely certain that No-Face had been looking at me through some kind of little peephole up in the roof. It seemed so real that I lay there a long time all shivery and clammy, curled up tight so he couldn't get a good view of me.

But this is crazy. You can't see me, No-Face — it's dark in here.

You're not going to make me paranoid or any of that stuff. Nothing you could do is going to send me over the edge. I've seen all those old horror movies. The wisps of smoke curling from secret vents, and real eyes looking through eyeholes in portraits. The villain hiding in the armor. You try looking at me through some kind of hole up there, and I'll stab your eyes out. Or something.

But if you are up there — is it to let me out? Finish

me off? Please, somebody. Come and help me. It's against the law to kidnap people. Is it against the law to get kidnapped? I'm sorry. I didn't mean to. If you could help me

No. Wait. Listen to this. Clackity-clack. Listen to me — do I sound scared, do I sound weak? Pounding away.

I have put the vase of flowers on the windowsill. Iris, with little orange tufts of hair. Dew on them. Spring and weddings. All that whiteness is full of color. I can't think of the word. Irra Irede Iridescent. How did all that beauty come from a root in the dark ground?

You see? Clackity-clack.

My father is blustery, sometimes. How is that for a descriptive word, Miss Flannery? He thinks he is not providing for his family. He is afraid my mom will say, "Why do I have to be the strong one?" All the money goes into house payments and clothes and food and insurance. And empty shampoo bottles and wrapping paper in the wastebasket and garbage and conferences with teachers this sentence isn't ending right, is it?

Doctors bring their Porsches in to be fixed, looking through him like he was a windowpane. They have people's lives in their hands, and they forget about changing oil.

He blusters at home, after work. At my mom. I guess he needs to. So he won't go back to Peewee's Automotive and flatten somebody rich with a cheater bar. Weird, though. He would trust me to a doctor who had a Porsche with bad brakes.

Great way to get revenge, Daddy. Marry me off to one of them.

This gets so hard. I give myself orders. Keep it light,

Jackie. Don't let the elevator music miss a beat — you never know who might be listening.

Then the quicksand slowly opens and swallows me up.

So, okay. I always said I wasn't going to ever get married. Too much can go wrong. So why clutter up my life with dreams, anyway? Clear out the closet. Pitch out the wonderful things I might have been. The good I might have done.

I have to be calm about the water. I know I've got to. Captain Bligh in the lifeboat forty-one days and all that. Only, didn't he have rain? I have to stay in control. I hold out, and wait, and don't touch it until I can't stand it any longer. But every time I give the jar a slosh it feels lighter. I stroke it. So fragile. Full of life. The food gets harder to force down. I can taste the mold. I count and re-count and calculate and plan. But what's the use? Do I starve now, or later? Dehydrate slowly, on in one final panic? I think, Drink it! Eat it! It's like an itch. One little dot on your skin itches and that's all you can think about. Your mind rivets on scratching.

I see liquids. I plan what I'll drink. Water. Just water. From the tap. Splashing, fizzing through that little thing on the faucet that turns it to bubbles. Or from a pitcher. The sound. The glass. Heavy. Tilting into my mouth. Down my throat. I can follow it all the way down, trickling. I think it even has a smell, like rain coming. Dew. Snow. Rivers. All that life pouring by. Dimples and ripples and swells and glints. I put my hand in it. I walk into it, over my head.

Please turn off the fountains. It's running in the gutters. Please don't do that. I would gladly drink your bathwater.

No-Face, if you are listening — I am going to stop now. Because I want to. I have other things to do. Still in control. Just stopping.

TTM

A long blank space in my mind. I have the feeling I said strange things.

I am calm now. So much better. I will try to be more systematic. Make sure the journal pages stay consecutive in the lid of the typing-paper box. A record for the grandkids. Only thing, they'll be busy keeping their own journals on their way out to the space station. My great adventure will be a big yawn.

I listen all the time. I hear my heart in the silence, and my gurgles and creaks. I think the ringing in my ears must be a soft continuous message from outer space, only I don't have the electronic equipment to translate it with. I wish I did. I might be hearing wonders. Answers to the questions. They have to be wise, out there. Surely they know they're not getting through to me, but they still keep sending. Just in case. The way

I hopefully kept saying, "Gillie — fetch!" until he understood.

I sing. Yes. Even songs without words. I sing ta-ta-ta TA-ta. The tango. I run my private videos. One has a haughty lady with spit curls on her cheeks, the man in black, both with those Spanish waistlines too slender to be true. They click, hold, click, pelvis-to-pelvis, with faces like Buster Keaton. They are absolutely matched, their steps are a drama. Are they hating, or loving, or testing each other? Or all three?

I hear my favorite sounds. Glasses clinking. My mom and dad putting plates and silverware into the dishwasher. Scraping pans. They have the most ordinary voices. Their pauses stretch as if they had all the time in the world.

The wind is moving. I see it from really far away, like the satellite pictures on weather maps, pushing clouds over the earth, curling and flowing. It passes through our oaks, and then palm trees, and over oceans and up cliffs of other places, the same wind. With my voice still in it, a teeny teeny noise lost in the roar of waves and blowing leaves.

Somewhere a little puff of air touches somebody's face and he sits bolt upright and exclaims in exasperation, "By Jove, we really must potter over to the Colonies and rescue that abominable girl, or teatime will be quite spoilt!"

I remember how Saturday sounds. The lawn mowers, the kid-voices. Car doors slamming and people off on errands or garage sales or visits. And always, over the other sounds, a little airplane droning, lazy, hazy, someone escaping into thin air.

I listen to Miss Flannery read aloud to us in class. She rolls the words like candies in her mouth to get the flavor. I'm glad she doesn't think we're too old to be read to. I'm glad she isn't ashamed to cry at the sad parts, and blow her nose.

I tell her all the fancy corny things I think of, that sound too sentimental to say to ordinary people. I ask her, "If you loved life, would it love you back — would a circle form?" She thinks awhile, and says, "It would. It does." I say, "And do you have to expect it to love you? Is it how you feel and act about it that makes the difference?" She nods, with that almost smile and says, "You may have found the secret."

THE STORY

"Where'd summer go?" Josh asked. They were sprawled at the edge of the garden, grubby and tired, on the day before school started again. They could feel the stillness of something ending.

"Seniors," Amy said, testing the word. "Can you believe it? Brain, get me through another year — please!"

"Are you addressing me?" Lynn asked, stretching.

Amy laughed. "Yeah, okay? So you give me a little friendly help when it's a report or something. But remember, I do the legwork."

"Is this because she has the legs for it?" Josh asked lazily.

Amy said, "But then Lynnie sits down and sort of puts it into deathless words for me — thank goodness."

114

"Is this because she has the seat for it?" Josh murmured. He came awake dodging as Lynn swung at him. "Hey, it's a neat seat!" He tried to pat it as Lynn scooted out of reach.

"Don't get my little friend started about her bottom," Amy warned. "She's got hang-ups."

"She's got the bottom of the barrel," Lynn said gloomily.

"See?" Amy told him, shrugging.

They finished the cans of pop they had brought with them, and put the empties back in the cooler to take to the truck.

"What do you two like best about each other?" Josh suddenly asked. "What's kept you a matched set all these years?"

"You mean besides the great results we get, pooling her brain and my charm?" Amy asked in mock innocence. She thought, and her voice got serious. "We filled up each other's blanks."

Lynn hesitated, struggling with something hard to confess. "I guess I was always afraid I wasn't, you know, enough of anything to matter. And Amy was always so — enough."

Amy smiled. "Yeah, she was a mess at first. So shy. But I was a mess in my way, too."

"Country Mouse meets City Mouse," Lynn agreed.

"What else?" Josh asked.

Lynn said, "Well, I liked it that she took risks. She was really full of life. And my folks liked it that she was a 'Nice Little New Friend Who Could Draw Me Out.' "

"We admired each other's talents," Amy said, warming up. "In fact, we were the first people to notice that we even had talents."

Lynn shrugged. "We just felt better and safer and everything when we were together. That's all."

Josh looked at Amy. "Is that all?"

Amy said, "She was trusting."

She got up and went to the tree with the hole in its trunk and got out the mosquito repellent. She brought it back to them.

"So how come you let me join the club?" Josh asked. "What did I have?"

"Maybe nothing," Lynn said, straight-faced to tease him. "Maybe each of us just THOUGHT you must be special if the other one of us liked you and wanted to be friends."

"You had a driver's license and could borrow a truck," Amy said. She smeared her legs with long lazy strokes.

Josh said, "Well, I'm glad I got to join. I know I'm just an honorary member — you've got so many things you want —"

"Hey," Lynn said, "the club got bigger, the plans got bigger, and you're part of it now — so don't keep saying that."

Amy took the bottle back to the tree. She climbed up and hung from a limb. "Can you believe a year from now we're going to be thinking college instead of life in Sickly Heights?"

Lynn turned, surprised. "We're going on the trip first."

Josh gazed at Amy. "Lawyers' little girls have to go to college. I think it's a law."

"The trip can be later, some summer," Amy said, dropping to the ground.

"But how long does it take to go around the world?" Lynn asked. "I mean — doesn't it take months?"

"Lynnie, you can go around the world in an airplane in hours."

"But I don't mean in a plane. I mean saving our money and going like we've been talking about. With bikes, and all."

Josh said, "How much money have you saved?"

She was silent. She had been baby-sitting twice a week all summer, but her savings were going to seem small compared to the money they had made. Josh had practically lived at Classy Grass, and Amy had fallen into a great baby-sitting job for a couple her dad knew, three or four times a week. Lynn had begged, "Ask if I can come help!" but Amy said, "That's the first thing they told me — no friends coming over."

Lynn said, "I haven't saved much. But if I get a job really soon —" She thought of something. "My grandmother might give me money for a graduation gift. She's been sort of hinting she will, if my grades go up."

"Promise her anything," Amy advised.

"We really are going to do it, aren't we?" she asked, feeling a little chill of uncertainty.

Josh and Amy smiled. Josh said, "Lynnie, we're going to do it. Trust us."

She let out a glad relieved breath, and went back to work. She opened three paper sacks and began to fill them with equal amounts of cucumbers, squash, and peppers. The thick mulch of grass clippings that Josh had brought out from his mowing jobs felt warm and giving under her bare feet. She could hear him behind her, grunting as he tugged up deep-rooted onions.

He said, "Amy says not so much for her this time — with her dad gone so much, things spoil." He looked around and sighed. Amy was gone. He swiped his hands clean against his shorts. "I guess it's my turn," he told Lynn, and went to find her.

Lynn kept gathering vegetables, listening with half her attention for their voices. In the golden haze the grasshoppers leaped away as she reached too close. She loved this still, sliding-into-evening time, but their days together always ended too soon.

Suddenly she heard laughter. Amy sprinted past the garden, sopping wet and squealing like a two-year old. Josh followed, trying to catch her. He stopped at the fence, laughing as she disappeared into the thicket.

"She was in the lake," he said, gasping for breath. "Lying with her head on a rock, letting minnows swim in and out of her clothes. I said we'd make a campfire with a spit — you know — and dry her on it, round and round."

"She's going to be cold when the sun goes down," Lynn said, sliding the sacks to the long corridor of bean vines. "You better keep her running till she dries." She knelt and crawled into the shadowy green tunnel.

"Hey, what are you doing?" Josh called. All the laughter had gone out of his voice.

"I'll bet there's a bushel of beans under here that we haven't been picking," she answered through the leaves.

Josh came closer. "Hey, get out of there," he said

uneasily. "There could be spiders and snakes and who-knows-what in all that mulch."

"Josh!" she exclaimed, scrambling out. "Somebody knows about our garden."

"Who?" he asked, holding his face blank.

"I don't know. A tramp. Little boys camping out. Somebody's slept in there. Like it's a big long tent."

"You're kidding," he said, and peeped in.

"There's extra grass piled up, and mashed into a hollow. Oh, I love it — what if it was an escaped convict or somebody running from the police, and he hid in our bean row."

She was startled to find Amy beside her, looking chilled in the stretching shadows.

Josh told Amy, "Other people get cutworms — we get convicts."

"Leave it to Lynnie," she agreed.

"Can't you picture it?" Lynn asked. "Him holed up in there, listening to the bloodhounds baying. Oh, wounded — he's wounded, but he crawls out in the dawn to take tomatoes and carrots back into his hideout."

Amy began to rub her arms. "I'm picturing it. But I'm also freezing. Can we start home?"

Josh said, "Serves you right. I still think rotating you slowly over a hot — " She ducked past him and looked into the bean tunnel. He laughed, watching her. "I hated to tell Lynnie that it just looked to me like a pile of mulch. What do you think?"

"Maybe a nest for a very big bird?" Amy straightened up and smiled at Lynn. "No, maybe you're right. You know what you've got to do? You've got to start traveling all around the country, like Johnny Appleseed, only planting beans with these crisscross pole things for them to climb on, so escaped prisoners can have a place to hide."

"Hey," Josh said, looking delighted, "you could go down in history, mouse. Lynnie the Bean Lady."

"I love it," she murmured as he gathered her close in one arm and Amy in the other, and guided them through the golden sunset to the truck.

That would be called the end of a chapter, wouldn't it, Miss Flannery? And real writers would stretch and have a ham sandwich and a glass of iced tea, go to the bathroom, maybe even take a little walk in the sunshine, and get back to work, right?

The bums.

I get so tired. It's hard to keep writing. I ache. I think about that French writer you told us about who used to close himself up in a room with a bottle of whatever he drank, and didn't come out until he had finished another book. I wonder if he had the feeling he was sort of unraveling himself like a sweater until he was all gone — but in his place was this pile of words with his life in them.

If I don't focus hard on writing I think about eating and drinking. I try not to. I try to think about people who are REALLY starving, really month-after-month starving until they feel their bodies breaking down to let their hearts and brains and vital things have any nourishment that's left. But I think of all that waste out there, all the good things growing out of the earth for us, and I can't understand.

I wish I had read more. So I'd have more things I could take out of my little mental filing cabinet, to fill the emptiness with.

I've thought about a lot of things here that I never took the time to think about before.

Maybe we ought to have compulsory kidnapping.

TTM

I went on a crying jag. Got myself pretty hysterical, I guess. When I woke up my face hurt, like I had gone bananas and tried to batter down a wall with my nose. I don't remember what I did. Maybe something pig-headed in me started yelling, "I'm not ending up in here!" and I started slamming myself into the concrete.

It's hard to admit there's been a time or two when I woke up and couldn't think where I was, or who I was. I don't like coming to with a skinned nose and dried blood in my hair — if that's what it is. Damn — when your mind doesn't work right, how can you trust anything?

The water's safe — I didn't knock over the jar. Oh, God, I could have. The idea gives me the chills. But the jar's okay. Nobody came in here while I was raving. My bakery shop on the steps hasn't been mashed. Nothing missing. The poop pile okay. I knew enough to leave THAT alone, even if I was crazy in the head.

Maybe I was dreaming something so real I acted it out. My dad said once my granddaddy had a nightmare that a burglar was in his house. It was so real he had grabbed one of those rubber plunger things from the bathroom and was whamming Grandma with it when he finally woke up.

It's weird to think how we go over the edge, mentally, every time we have a bad dream or a big shock. Doing in a small way what people do who go over the edge and don't come back. I mustn't get that close.

There is nothing wrong with my mind. It's just working different. Is this what they call hallucinating? I never did it before, so how can I know? Wild. It's nice, sometimes. I saw little boys, golden-haired. Peaceful. They were in the sandbox.

Nothing's slipped. I can spell my name. Remember birthdays. Telephone numbers. Pledge of Allegiance to the Flag. The seven dwarfs and eight tiny reindeer — and the ten most beautiful women on TV.

Not the Ten Commandments, though. Sorry. Not the countries of Africa.

I'm just saying things. I'm like Scheherazade telling stories. I have to keep writing to stay alive.

But who am I trying to kid? When the water goes, so do I. That will be it. I'll just stop, like a refrigerator going off. No little humming sound of life. No light inside.

Maybe that was what I was raging against in my dream when I tried to break down the wall with my face.

It gets bad to think about. I don't know how long

people can live without water. Or if it's horrible. Does your tongue swell up, and your skin shrivel? Does your blood get too thick to circulate? I know people die in deserts. But that's a combination of heat and exhaustion and stress and all. Miss Flannery told us once that when she was in Scotland she toured a castle and down in the dungeon there was this worn spot where prisoners had licked a cracked stone that was letting water seep in.

I don't want to be found looking gruesome like those horror movies, like I'd clawed the wall, screaming, or anything. I hope you go into a coma or something and keep a little dignity.

It doesn't make sense. Why can't it make sense? If there's not going to be any rules, I can't handle this.

I will get out of here, No-Face, I will live through this I am being rescued I am being found. You are breaking and telling. I will outlast you. Three police cars are screaming down the highway and you're in the first one between two officers and at each crossroad they give you a poke with a .38 Special until at one road you say, "Turn," and the lights are flashing and the sirens are howling, closer and closer.

I wonder who you are. What do you look like — what kind of thoughts do you have? Can people look at you and guess that you kidnapped a girl off the street? Is there a reason why you can do an awful thing like that? Did an awful thing ever happen to you?

If you're asking for a ransom, and get it, how will you spend the money? Will you think of me when you spend it? My folks will raise it, somehow. Sell the house, car, everything. Borrow it from people. Mr. Beckner. Wouldn't that be ironic, if it's really April you think you've got?

I slept. So deep, so heavy. Head like a cantaloupe.

Someone came. It was very nice. We talked. Then we went up the mountain. I acted like I knew how to do it. Fell down some, but pretended to be brave.

My mom knows something happened. Not what it was, because I didn't tell. But she was driving east of town and she said, "How about we pick some of your famous veggies while we're this close?" And I didn't know what to say to stop her. She drove out to the lake and around to the garden and there was everything knocked down. Mashed. A total wreck. She just got out, really quiet, and stood by the fence. Then she got a sack out from under the seat and began to gather the wilted peppers that were still on the broken-down bushes, and pick the tomatoes and beans that hadn't been trampled.

She said she'd heard that onion tops needed to be crushed down, anyway, to make the bottoms grow bigger.

I said it was a pity people don't grow bigger when they get stomped.

She nodded. She put a pile of bruised cucumbers in the sack, and said, "Always salvage what you can."

I want to go home.

Who was the explorer who didn't make it back from the Antarctic — left the notes? And years later they found canned goods in the ice, still edible. No. Think I'm remembering two different expeditions. One South Pole, one North. I'm not making it up, though. Ask someone at the library.

His name was Scott. Richard? Robert. The last entry said, "This is so sad."

DEAR MOM AND DAD,

I am fine. Sorry I haven't kept those cards and letters coming. But I could complain that you don't write back to me, couldn't I? I hope you are keeping your spirits up, and expecting miracles.

Don't take this wrong, but I wish you had told me more about God. I guess when it's something that personal you don't just come right out with it, but I always felt you had some kind of deep strong belief. The same way I always sensed — even when you were ticked off at me and at your wits' end about what to do — that you still loved me completely. It's hard to explain.

Anyway, I tune into something that seems really powerful and near, sometimes, and I don't know if it's coming from you, or it's other people's good thoughts, or if it's from something else that loves me, too, and wants me to know.

It makes me think of Donna and David from down the road. Always telling us how good God was to them, giving them signs what to do, and all, and how they said they'd pray for us when we told them we were moving into town. I felt so embarrassed. And now I wish I had asked them more about it, how they got that way.

I don't want my life to be like a weed — appear, grow till frost comes, then plop, fall over.

But on the other hand, if you look at a weed, it seems so content being what it is, sort of intense and single-minded. Glad, even. It doesn't go around making empty small talk, or buying fad clothes, or wondering who to believe. Does it know something I don't know?

With mysteries, you keep turning them over in your mind. You know? They're not like factual things where you say, "Well, that's that," and let them drop out of your head all finished.

Does life seem mysterious so we'll keep struggling to figure it out?

I like the idea of something out there being really tremendously good and perfect and complete. Maybe there is.

Maybe not. But if you acted as if it was there and you wanted to be a part of it, then you'd live a different way, wouldn't you? You'd sort of keep it in mind as a model, and not want to fall short. So it wouldn't matter if it really existed or not, would it, as long as you thought it did and acted as if it did?

Or take a lamp. It's not going to light up until you plug it into the socket where the power is. You don't have to understand how the power works. But you do have to believe it's there in the wall, waiting to work, and you do have to plug in.

This is a weird letter. It's taken me forever to write. Shaky hands. Like Gillie scratching himself in his sleep.

I guess I got off on a strange idea. But there's got to be some meaning to this. I need somebody wise to explain it. Show me how it makes sense. Because if it doesn't, why am I going through all this?

I'm really weak now. I need to stop. I know you love me and are doing all you can. Don't blame yourselves that things aren't going better.

Love,
Jackie

THE STORY

Amy's dad called just as Lynn was starting out the
door on a Saturday afternoon. School had started two
weeks before, and she was on her way to the library to
work on a report. He asked for Amy.

"She's not here," Lynn told him.

"Oh?" he said, sounding as mildly curious as he ever
let himself. "I understood she was spending last night
with you."

"You must have misunderstood each other," she said,
in a hurry to go.

"She doesn't seem to be at home," he said. "I tried
there last night and this morning. I'm calling from out
of town."

"She could be at the library," Lynn said carefully.
"We're supposed to meet there. You want me to tell her
to call you?"

"That won't be necessary, thank you, Lynn," he said curtly. He hesitated, and in her mind she saw him adjust his tie. "Actually, Lynn, I'd like to mention something that concerns both you girls. I appreciate that you make Amy so welcome in your home, but she almost lives there, and the burden on your parents —"

"Well, not this summer," Lynn said. "Not since she got that special baby-sitting job. She hardly —"

"But several nights a week and weekends is too much," he went on. "I'm going to ask her to limit her sleepovers and I'd like you to back me up. Will you?"

She could see his handsome calculated smile in her mind.

He filled in the space her silence was leaving. "I'm going to be able to have more time at home myself now, and I think Amy and I ought to get to be better friends. Will you help me out, Lynn?"

"Yes, sir," she murmured. She tried to calm her flurry of reactions. He'd broken up with his lady friend, it sounded like. Maybe that was good. But he'd just said that Amy had been sleeping over at Lynn's most of the summer. That was bad. Because she hadn't.

"Good girl!" he said warmly, and hung up.

She looked at her fingers clenched on the receiver, and slowly forced them loose. What had she done? She hadn't lied. She had simply protected Amy, automatically and without any questions, by not saying anything.

She checked to see if her folks were still in the kitchen, too busy to have heard. Her heart was pounding fast. She called Amy's house, letting the phone ring time after time as she whispered, "Be there!" She called Classy Grass and asked for Josh.

"You know where Amy is?" she asked.

He said, "Sure, she's just come by. I'm finishing up for the day, so — aren't we all meeting at the library?"

Lynn drew a deep breath. "Would you tell her I need to talk to her?"

"Now?" Josh asked. "Where? Library? Your house?"

Lynn looked around. "The garden."

There was silence a moment. "Sure," Josh said.

Lynn hung up and smoothed the apprehension from her face. She leaned in at the kitchen door to tell her folks she was meeting the kids at the lake. Slowly she pedaled off on her bike. She needed a long ride. She had hard things to think about.

As she got closer she went slower, wishing she would never get there. She didn't expect to arrive first if Amy caught a bus near Classy Grass, but she felt no surprise when she glimpsed the truck parked in the little road that led to the garden, and saw Josh standing beside Amy.

They walked to the fence where Lynn propped her bike. "What's up?" Amy asked brightly.

"I don't know," Lynn said. "I just needed to talk to you." She looked at Josh.

"Hey," he said. "I'll wait in the truck."

"Why?" Amy asked. "It's all for one and one for all and stuff like that, isn't it?" She smiled at Lynn. "So, what's your problem?"

Lynn stared into her waiting face, unable to start.

Josh said, "You sounded so intense — I told Amy

maybe your grandmother had just sent you a ticket for around the world."

Lynn turned her strained face to his. Warily she said, "As a matter of fact, she wrote me a letter. She said she had decided to help with my college expenses. And I wrote back—" She felt a dropping sensation as their eyes gazed into hers. "I said, thanks, but I was going on a long trip with my friends and I thought an experience like that was better preparation for life than college."

"That was dumb," Amy murmured. "Couldn't you have said the trip could be after college, or during?"

"So?" Josh asked.

"So—I don't know. She didn't answer my letter— she wrote my mom. And my mom threw a raving fit, yelling what did I SAY to her—how could I mess up such a wonderful chance? Not even giving me time to explain. She just kept saying how much help it would have been, and all that." Lynn shrugged, surprised at how evenly the words were pouring out past the turmoil inside. "So I guess her deal's off."

"Dumb," Amy repeated in regret.

"Why? It's how I felt." She whirled on Josh. "We ARE going, aren't we?"

He looked at Amy. "Sure we are."

"Because if we aren't—" She swallowed a lump of fear.

"Then you blew it, didn't you?" Amy said softly. She flicked a grasshopper off Lynn's shoulder. "So you blew it, Lynnie. Something else will come along. Things come to you."

133

"That's not true," Lynn said following in surprise as Amy started into the thicket beside the lake.

"You always had everything so easy," Amy said, going faster. "Your folks, and love, and Josh — and you KEEP everything, hang on to it — you're going to have it all. The big dreams, and us, and whatever you want."

Lynn stopped, rigid with amazement. "Hey, you've got what I've got — my folks love you — you've got a home to come to whenever you want to."

Amy said, "No. I have it because you give it. Because you're nice."

"What's that got to do with anything?" She felt Josh take her elbow as she stumbled.

"Nothing. Forget it," Amy called back from the thicket's shade. "So you pissed off your granny — is that what you were in such a hurry to tell me?"

"No. It's not. Your dad called me. Looking for you."

"Oh?" Amy said, with the same little lilt her dad used. "Where's he — Timbuktu?"

"He thought you'd spent the night at our house. Because you weren't at home."

"Oh, great," Amy said with a laugh. "So he's split with what's-her-name and suddenly recalls he has this daughter back in town."

"He thinks you've been spending a lot of your time at our house, Amy."

"I have."

"Not this summer. You haven't. You've been busy. Really busy. Nearly every time I asked."

"I have been busy," Amy said. "What's the deal?"

"Well, the deal is, I didn't know what to say to your dad."

Josh asked, "What did you say?"

"Nothing. Because I thought — I thought Amy could explain what this is all about."

Amy stopped and turned on them. "Well, I can't. I don't have to. If you can't trust me after all these years —"

"Amy, I trust you." Her throat closed up. How could they be talking to each other this way? "But if you're using my folks, and lying to your dad — don't I deserve to know why?"

Josh said, "She's trying to tell you, Lynnie."

She shook her head. "No, she isn't."

"She's been wanting to, a long time," he said. "It's a hard thing to explain. We love each other, Lynnie."

"I know we do. That's why we ought to be able to talk to each other without —"

She stopped. She felt her mind shift with a jolt. She forced her eyes to move like a searchlight over their taut faces.

"Lynnie." Josh took her shoulders in his hands. "Amy and I. We love each other. Not the way the three of us do."

She felt herself sink under water into a quivering heaviness, and then fight her way up through the pressure until she could catch a breath. "Get away from me," she whispered, twisting out of his grasp.

"Lynnie," Amy said from her patch of weeds, "what did you expect? Staying friends forever is not what happens."

"Why?" she asked in her strangled voice. "My mom has friends she made in kindergarten. My dad has Army buddies —"

"Lynnie, Josh and I didn't want to be Army buddies!"

Josh tried to take her arm. She jerked away. "Don't," she warned.

"You were making all the rules," Amy said. "You couldn't see how it was with us. We didn't have anybody. We needed each other."

"You had me!"

Josh said, "Don't we still have you? We want to still have you. We love you."

"It wasn't hurting you when Josh and I were together," Amy said. "What we were doing didn't change how we felt about you."

"Doing?" she asked, dazed. A cramp of dread took her breath.

"Can't we still be friends?" Josh begged. "Jesus, if I'm causing this —"

"Doing?" Lynn repeated in a dream-voice. "You mean all those times you were busy?" She turned on Amy. "All the baby-sitting? All those nights you weren't staying over at my house?"

"Lynnie, not ALL those nights," Josh protested. "Jesus."

"How long?" she asked. "All summer?"

Amy carefully braced her hands against a twisted little tree. Its leaves quivered. "Since the skit," she said. "Okay? Because it was a special time, the success and the applause, and we didn't want it to end."

Josh said, "Lynnie, her dad forgot to come by. So I took her home."

Lynn walked away blindly. She felt the dry branches hit her face, but there was no place in her consciousness for the added pain. Dimly she heard Amy's voice say, "Stop her, Josh." She began to stumble faster, in a blur of desolation.

Josh came behind her. "Lynnie, we wanted to tell you. But we knew you'd be like this. We didn't want to hurt you."

She whirled to face him. "You came out HERE, didn't you? You laughed with me about escaped convicts and Johnny Appleseed, and all the time it was you."

"Lynnie, it was a happy place. We didn't —"

"That wasn't fair!" she yelled. "That was cruel. Pretending, all these months. Making a fool out of me. Why couldn't you have been honest and just told me?"

"Lynnie, we've just told you. We're trying to be honest."

"Where else?" she demanded, dizzy with hate. "Your house, her house, the truck — what other happy places — and then playing games with me, all smiling and innocent!"

"We weren't smiling and we weren't innocent," Josh yelled back. "Don't make it sound easy for us, damn it. We love you. Amy loves you. You two have got to stay best friends. Please, Lynnie, if I thought I'd ruined that —" He held out his hands, pleading. "Say you'll stay friends. It's up to you."

"Me?" she exclaimed. "You two do whatever you damn please and I'm supposed to take it?"

He said, "You don't have to take it, or like it. But how much you hate us or how much you let us hurt you IS up to you."

Amy came closer through the brush. "Lynnie?" she asked. "Please, can't you be reasonable about this?"

"Oh, sure." She backed away defensively. " 'Give me

137

just one more little reassurance, Lynnie' — right?" Her hands shot out, warning them out of her space. "Damn — no. I've spent half my life taking your side, and covering for you, and hauling you out of your moods. At my house we were always thinking what if she did something — really did something —"

"That's not fair," Josh said.

"You like being a victim, Amy!" she rushed on, unable to stop. "You're still blaming your mother for that one bad time. Listen, I know people need help and can't do things alone, but you have to change inside. You can't make a career out of letting us comfort you and fix your life for you. THAT'S not fair."

"Lynnie," Amy begged. "Don't be like this." She began to cry as Lynn backed away through the brush. "We've got to stay friends. We've got too many plans. We've got the trip."

"Damn the trip," Lynn said.

"But, Lynnie, we want you to come with us!" She tried to catch Lynn's arm.

Lynn jerked herself free. "God, do you think I'd travel with you the way you just said it? Not 'We're all still going to see the world together.' Didn't you hear yourself? You were saying, 'Sure, Lynnie, YOU can come with US.' Wow, thanks, Miss Generosity — I'm overwhelmed."

She found herself running, lurching and tripping in her rush to leave them behind. The edge of the lake appeared so suddenly that she was sinking into mud before she could stop. She veered off, fell over a rock, and rushed on along the muddy edge, limping in despair.

From a distance she heard Josh call, "Come back, Lynnie. We can't leave you out here."

She kept moving through the tangled undergrowth. All she wanted was for them to go so she could stop.

"Don't be like this — this is stupid!" Amy called.

She went on. As she freed herself from a thorny bramble, she saw from the corner of her eye that they were talking together.

Finally Josh called, "We've got to go, Lynnie. If you don't come we're going to call your dad at the first phone, so he can come and get you."

"I have a bike!" she told them in her mind. "I'm not dead. I can get home when I'm ready." She walked faster.

When she looked back at last, they were gone.

She sat down in the weeds and let the sobs come tearing out of her throat. She had been simpleminded and blind and innocent. Trusting. Stupid! She hated herself. She hated them in their nest between the bean rows, smoothing mosquito repellent on each other's naked skin, going eagerly into a world they had wanted to know without her. Leaving her behind.

It was almost dark when she got up, and went back to the garden. She pulled up the tomato stakes and trampled everything — peppers and squash, cucumbers, the feathery asparagus that had been there before they had made their Eden around it. She toppled the beanpoles and crushed the vines, kicking and stomping, still gasping out things she hadn't said to their faces.

When she heard the car she calmed herself and went out the gate into the road. Her dad looked around in the near-dark.

"Troubles?" he asked. She had no idea what they had told him. She let him pull her against his chest for a moment. But as the crushing weight in her own chest began to take her breath she stepped back out of the circle of his arm.

She sat in the car while he tied the bicycle to the roof rack.

When he got in beside her he lifted her fingers to his face. "You smell like mashed tomato leaves," he said. "I always loved the smell of tomato leaves." Then he took her home.

TTM

Feels like I went through a long cycle in a washing machine. My bones ache. I am so tired. But I needed to finish what I was writing. I feel calm, now. Drained, I guess is the word. But glad that I worked my way through to the end.

I've been sitting here holding the little note I found in my raincoat pocket. It's folded five-sided, the way April and I always did it, so we would recognize our messages to each other. I keep wanting to open it and read it, and have it answer all my questions.

The injured part of me keeps asking, "Was it something April had written? Was it a love note to Zack, folded our way? Was it about me?"

It could be a note I wrote and forgot. A poem, my secret thoughts to share with April. Did they read it and laugh together? I let myself hold it and hurt.

I want to hurt. I want to turn the pain around and around, feeling its corners — wondering what its message is.

I feel very stupid. Childish. Very deceived and small and crushed down. Jackie-in-the-Box.

I took the one earring that had been left in my backpack, and dropped it through the little grill into the drain. We're not a matched set anymore, April.

I've been sick again. Doubled up with cramps that knock me out and let me come back again. My knees and elbows are scraped. Like I'd crawled on the floor around and around. Fingernails broken.

Ate something with raisins in it. Cinnamon smell. Good. Licked the wrapper. If a mold can live on it, so can I, right?

Afraid I'll grab up everything that's left and stuff it in my mouth.

Can't.

Why not. Finish everything. Turn loose.

I can't.

Please don't do this. I've hung on so long, not asking for it to be easy, haven't I?

ZACK,

This time it's harder than ever to know how to start.

Maybe picture some grand old lady in a canopied bed, worn out and sad. People gathered around. Faithful maid in tears. Background music, good spare dialogue. She wants to settle her affairs. But what she keeps getting are blurred slow-motion flashbacks of sweet happier times.

I know — I'm still being artificial with you. Protecting myself. Keeping my distance, the way I always did, so I wouldn't break our rules.

I'm not really sure what I feel. Hate, as far as I can tell.

No, other things, too. Still a lot of grief. And regret for all the changes. The three of us mattered so much. Playing the game fair was important to me. I tried to keep it honest and balanced out — you know I did.

But one of you, or both of you, didn't play fair. I tear myself up wondering which one of you persuaded the other one to go along. Somebody had to be first.

But I guess I don't want to know.

I won't apologize for how I reacted. I said angry things. What I did to the garden was ugly and wrong. But I only ruined something that had been ruined for me.

I guess I never knew you, Zack. At least I never knew when you were real. You're a good actor. Of all the people in the world, I had to pick two actors for my dearest friends.

If you hadn't known how to hide the truth so well, I might have guessed at the beginning, and it wouldn't have built up to so much hurt.

I guess the sad old lady in this scene had trouble all her life giving up anything, or anybody. It breaks her heart to give up someone she loved. To give him up to someone ELSE she loved, and lose them both — that was doubly hard. It didn't leave her much.

Maybe her problem was that she had the idea she was helpless. Who was she to change the world? Or even change herself? Somebody else, or something else, always had the power.

It's been that way with me, too. I always seemed to be living this sort of beige-colored skimpy little life. It was a jolt to me to find out April was jealous of how good it was. And another jolt that she had to take something out of it for her very own. Somebody.

I couldn't see why. To me she had always been this, you know, FLOWER blossoming away like crazy, while I was this fingernail having to be pushed out into the world. It's strange to realize now that we were just

144

these two dumb kids growing up scared, each one of us expecting the other one to provide what was missing.

I really leaned a lot on her. And then on you, too, Zack. I was so grateful to have you guys and trust you that I practically turned myself over to you so you could lead my life for me. It's taken a real clunk on the head to force me to admit what I've been doing.

But being in here has really changed all that. In here, if I lean on anything it's a concrete wall. So I'm trying hard to imagine myself a new way. I'm trying to imagine all those people out there doing all sorts of things — because of me. The police. My relatives. Even strangers praying for me and stuff. I've changed lives. Me. I've got the power.

I had it with my folks — even starting before I was born. I'd never thought about all those years they were arranging their lives to include me. I only noticed things like my dad giving up the place he loved for my "Advantages." And my mom getting what she wanted because she had me for an excuse.

I've changed you and April, too, Zack. You have me in you whether you like it or not. As long as you have memories, I'm there. Friends do that to each other.

I remember thinking you were something wonderful that just came in and started rearranging our lives. You and those big hands and coat-hanger shoulders and new ways of seeing things — suddenly you were showing us how much bigger and better friendship could be. So you changed us, that way. Me, for sure. And you're still pushing us into new shapes, aren't you?

Now I've seen another side of you that hurt me a lot to see. Okay. I know you never said you were anything

145

but an ordinary boy, as capable as anybody of doing easy second-rate things. It wasn't your fault that I made you more than you were. But all this takes time to get used to.

Maybe you're thinking the same thing. April said you'd dropped out of school — you're on your way to something else. That seems like another easy stupid thing to do, Zack, but I'm trying to understand how you feel. All those things you said to April and me about getting out of our lives and letting us be free to follow our dreams — I think you actually meant them, and did love us, and felt protective. And then when other feelings got in the way, you really struggled with the conflict in your heart. But a part of me can't help wondering if you saw this matched-set situation getting more complicated than you're ready for. You know? So complicated that you've just got to move on to something simpler. And easier for you. I guess I can't blame you. But if I'm right about this, it means April is going to be left behind again, doesn't it?

Be careful with her, Zack. She's not as tough as she seems. In fact, now that I really think about it, she's probably as innocent in her own way as I've been.

Sorry. Got dizzy and had to rest. It's hard to keep my thoughts focused.

Or maybe my problem is that I've been focusing too long on things I'm just beginning to understand. Whichever it is, a long time has passed and nobody is finding me.

I don't know what my chances are. I never thought I'd say that, but I guess the uncertainty has always been here inside, like one more cramp, only clutching at my head instead of my stomach. I'm living in a big crazy riddle, and I don't know how to solve it.

I keep thinking if I could only be OUTSIDE, seeing, talking, but wouldn't the riddle be the same — the same mystery of what we're here for, why we hurt each other, what comes after this? I'd just be more distracted by people and noise and all the input and feelings that were pushing me back and forth. I still couldn't be sure I was any more free or in control of my life than I am in here, could I? What if being free and in control is what I decide it is? What if it's up to me to say?

I blamed April for not being able to take charge of her life from inside herself. I guess I didn't realize how hard it is to grow that way, knowing nobody can help you or do it for you.

Maybe I have grown a little, in here. Right now it seems like crossing over from being a child to being an adult is about the most important step in a person's life. Maybe that's what I'm trying to do — so I can finally take charge of me.

I don't know what's going to happen to this new me, Zack. I haven't given up. But I have to be realistic. "Get real," you always told me. So I've been wondering. Like what I'd say if I left a will or something. Which is pretty dumb, because what have I got? How could I leave you something that I don't own? But I guess I'd say: to Zack I leave the garden. It's not in great shape, thanks to me, but gardens know how to start over, year after year. So ask my dad how to feed the asparagus. Take care of the apple tree, and help it live a long time.

Do you remember when we climbed up and sat in

the branches, close to the lightning, not even thinking how dangerous it was? Remember how the wind blew and how we held on for dear life?

Don't let April do all the hurting while you do all the running.

I'm sorry I hung up on you, every time you called. I was hurt and angry and confused, myself. I thought we had already said everything there at the edge of the lake.

Jackie-and-the-Beanstalks

I broke the water jar. The water's gone.
Not real. Shock makes it seem

My mind says, Pretend you're dreaming this.
Jar was safe against the wall. But I passed out. Standing there, then all at once felt myself falling. Heard myself. Lunged for a wall somewhere to brace against, knocked the jar over, going down. When I came to I could feel wetness under my cheek, soaking into the floor. Pressed bread slices into it, trying to keep it. What will I do, God? Help me. This hellhole place drank up my water.

Oh please let me be dreaming. Glass is scattered. Wet dust smell. My leg hurts. Soppy stuff is blood, I guess. I wrapped the raincoat sleeve around

I don't have any water.

Just want to lie in a ball on the floor forever, and not have to wonder what to do.

There is dynamite hidden behind the TV. I can blow up whatever I need. But isn't it dangerous?

Don't even know if you can use matches to light a fuse. I think they do in old movies. Throw it at the train. In funny movies, throw it at bumbly character. He pitches it back. Everybody in panic. Nobody blows up. Ever.

Do I need a match? That other thing. Detonator. Smoosh. Little plunger. What a risk, though. The destruction.

I don't think I have all this straight.

We ate on the porch. By the grapevine. I want to go home but why can't I?

When I am better?

I heard my name. Voices so clear that I woke up calling out, "I'm here, Daddy — in here."

I must have been out a long time. It's good to have my mind back.

I put the broken glass in the spider corner. My leg throbs, but the blood is dry. I'm not as weak.

I know this is serious. Either I'm being given a terrible test, or this is it.

Are you testing, out there?

You think you have me in your power, don't you? You think I'll lie here and dry up like an earthworm on the sidewalk.

You didn't think I'd eat that damp bread, but I did.

This is hard to take. What am I doing wrong?

I thought things happened so we could change. Learn. Grow. But if I don't get out of here to be different, after all of this, what was the purpose?

Oh, God, you know I want to live. I was just getting the hang of it.

Okay. People die too soon every day. They even die inside concrete walls — pillboxes, bomb shelters, tunnels, delousing rooms. Ways that are horrible and shocking. I am trying to be reasonable. What makes me special, right? They say forty thousand children a day die from diseases we could eliminate. Some things go beyond reason.

I want to be hopeful. I have been hopeful, haven't I? But there have been so many times before when I was so sure of good coming — winning a part in a play, or getting Gillie back. Or Zack and April and me. And then in spite of believing, it didn't come. Was there a reason why it didn't, or didn't I believe hard enough?

So, do you die young because you're all finished and ready and don't realize it? You've learned what you were supposed to learn, and done what you were here to do, and one day a truck runs you over and you're promoted to the next grade or whatever. You look down on all the weepy people. You say, "Hey, celebrate. I was in Honors Class all along and didn't know."

Dear Donna and David,
I could use one of your double-barreled prayers.

I wish I could stop crying. I try to stop. Just dry sobs, now. No tears. Need my tears.

Dear God,
I am very scared.
I wish I could tell you how I feel, without being so on guard. I mean, there's always that question looming, separating us: If you know about me, and love me, why is this happening?
Maybe you could ask me the same question.

DEAR NO-FACE,

Ronnie. Thurmond. Whoever you are. With the different names and the stale smell. With the grungy van. With my life in your hands.

This is hard, but I need to say something to you. I want to thank you for the food and water. It's gone now. The water's a cold damp spot on the floor. The food's in me. Gone. The last crumb. Because I decided. I get to say.

You didn't have to leave it in here. You didn't have to give me any help. I would just like for you to know I'm grateful for the time you gave me.

And also, thank you for what you didn't do that night. You know. When I was helpless and you could have.

When this first happened I wanted to get out of here and get my revenge. I wanted you punished. Written off. Dropped into a trash can for the garbage truck.

Maybe you were paid to do what you did, or duped some-way, but you chose to do it, and I wanted you locked up FOREVER for it, in a little dark scary cell so you'd know what you had taken from me and what you had made me go through.

I wanted you dead. You committed a crime, and a crime has to be balanced by something.

But I don't know what kind of something. Balancing it with another hurtful thing doesn't seem like the way to make progress, does it?

So now I take back what I thought. I don't want you dead. Dead stops all the possibilities. I don't have the time to waste, thinking destructive things.

What it boils down to is that I wouldn't want anybody to live like this, in the dark. I think you already know about the dark.

So I hope somebody —   How do I say this? I'm trying to wish help for you, Ronnie. Instead of justice.

If going on living gives us a chance to do better, how can I ask it for me and not ask it for you?

APRIL,

I couldn't look back at you there at the lake edge. I was glad when you were gone. I wanted to feel cold and furious and betrayed.

What is not-being-friends supposed to feel like? Does something actually die?

All the way back into town I could almost feel the waves of hate passing between us. I stared out the window, remembering all the things you and I had shared. The things we'd revealed to each other about ourselves and our folks — all the private unguarded things I'd told you. And now you were somebody I didn't know anymore.

That day you took all your things away, you said you wanted me out of your life. You said I ruined things. You were acting so crazy, I should have realized that you were desperate to hit out at somebody. It couldn't

155

be Zack, even if it was what he'd just told you that had set you off.

So it was me. It's okay. It's taken me a while, but I can see now that I was doing the same thing, there at the lake. Yelling cruel things. I had to hit back, too, before I could begin to grieve for the way things had been, and then turn loose and let you go on.

I wish you could turn loose, too, April. I know you have already, with me. But I mean turn loose of Zack. You're going to think I'm saying this out of jealousy. I'm trying not to. Looking back at the way you were acting at my house that day, I see now that I should have realized he had already broken off with you. I'm sorry for what you're going through, if it's true.

I think when he was talking about our big dreams, he had some even bigger dreams of his own. If they're burning him, you might as well face it — nothing's going to keep him from giving them a chance before he gets himself too tangled up to try.

I wish neither one of you needed the other one. I wish neither of you had ever expected the other one to make all your troubles go away. To me, what you've been doing seems really dumb and dangerous — it's like you were asking for trouble. But I'm not you. I'm just me, seeing it all from where I am.

I wish you could find some kind of a distance to look at it from, too. Maybe it would help.

Had to rest a little while. But I'm okay now.

I need to ask you for a favor. Please help my folks. If — just if — I happen not to be found until it's too late, it's going to nearly kill them. They'll think they failed me. Please be handy for talking or listening or crying or blaming, or whatever they need to do.

I guess people always think they'll have plenty of time to grow wise and see things clearer, and gradually everything will work out and be the way it ought to be. I guess we have to think we're in control of our lives, even while something like this is happening and we're being picked up like babies and carried into strange new rooms.

I thought I'd have time. Even while I waited in here I thought I'd be given back so much time that I'd manage to heal up from what's happened to us, and maybe we'd even be a part of each other's lives again. On a different level, I mean. Not with all the old plans and hopes that depended on each other. Not two little scraggly vines twined together for support. We'd have to go off in our own separate directions. The way you started off, I guess, when you chose Zack. We'd each climb the wall to whatever we wanted to reach — but with little shoots going out to one another, like fingers touching. Till finally we'd be two creaky old ladies exchanging pictures of our grandkids.

Or am I still being too innocent, asking for that? Right now all I want is to protect myself and not feel anything but numbness toward you.

But I can't be sorry we were friends. I guess that's how I can leave it if I have to. Being glad.

We did have fun, didn't we? Laughed more than we cried. Believed in each other.

Thanks for helping me get through the scary parts.

Anyway, all that stretching-into-eternity time, that I was expecting to have, is more like a big question mark now. Thinking about it sends me off into a kind of stillness. Something so intense is happening that my mind shuts a door on it. I guess you felt that way, the first time with Zack. I felt it at the lake when you told me. I guess we both felt it while I was being carried off in the van and you were standing in the street watching me go.

Scary corners to turn.

All my life, I guess, I've been afraid of changes and what they'd take from me. I wanted everything safe and permanent and explained. I tried not to think about things that didn't have answers. Like dying or anything deep like that. But actually when you look right at it, dying's not all that earth-shaking. It happens every second, to grass and people and insects and sounds and everything lucky enough to have lived.

So I'm trying not to be scared anymore. I know changes are how we grow. I accept that there are things that can't be explained by facts and figures. Maybe aren't even supposed to be.

I wanted facts when I found myself in here. I yelled questions. It wasn't fair to be faced with so much mystery.

But right now all the questions about where I am, and why, and what may become of me, don't really seem any more mysterious than where Zack is at this moment, or whether my folks will stay together, or what is going to happen to you.

I'm more curious than afraid now. My life's been so full, and there's still so much to learn and do — so much world out there to get to know — that I wish I could live a long time. And not have to think about endings until I've done all the things and loved all the people and felt all the feelings. I just can't accept that the pile of typed paper here in this lid is going to be all that's left of me and what I meant to be.

But guess what, April. I can do something without you. I've done this, and I can do the rest. If I have to.

I need to stop now. It takes forever to poke the keys and push the carriage return. Like trying to run in waist-deep water.

Keeps me off the streets, though.

So, if I don't see you again, and this is all I get to say, do some wonderful things with your life. Grow a lot. You have so many choices. Remember you've been chosen by a lot of people to be somebody special in their lives.

And remember me. Okay?

Your friend,
Jackie

So dizzy. But got the place tidy. Journal in lid of typing paper box. Took a while. So cold it's hard to move. Floor still damp so I put down pretend rug. Better. Maybe tomorrow, chairs. Should have thought sooner.

Bad times. Easier when I'm drifting in and out. At first I had periods when I felt strong. I was sun breaking through clouds. Now I feel blurred all the time. It's hard to concentrate. I've held out so long I would almost rather just let go. So it's weird trying to hang on and turn loose at the same time. I hunt for a place midway, sort of numb and still, and wait there.

But damn, the box is still more than half full of unused paper. I can't leave it blank, can I?

Burns me up to think some of these plastic wrappers have bits of mold in them that might outlive me.

I'm sorry, Miss Flannery, if it should turn out I've spent my last days writing about misunderstandings and resentments. I meant to make better use of my time and leave you a story about loving.

Did I create this? Did I do all this by myself? To myself? That's too scary to think about. It's like in those folk tales when somebody uses up his third wish before he realizes what he's done.

So, was it all meant to teach me something I might have learned easier if I had just been willing to?

Learned one thing the hard way. I can't get out of this place by myself. I can hang on like lint — I can believe in miracles — but I can't keep life going by myself. Right? Somebody out there has to keep believing, too, and searching for me.

I can't help you do that — it's up to you, like Zack said.

Unless my believing keeps you believing.

DEAR MOM AND DAD,

Don't get crazy, now. I want to say good-bye. Just in
case. We're cutting it close here, with the time. But I
know you have done everything. Everything you could.
If the miracle comes, and you find me, we'll laugh over
this letter, or maybe cry, and then we'll celebrate. But
I need to write it, just in case.

I thought you might give April any of my things you
don't want to keep. We loaned things back and forth so
much, nobody remembers who owned what, anyway.
Any clothes that fit, unless she doesn't like the idea of
wearing them.

If Miss Flannery would like some of my stories and
stuff, that's fine. But not to show anybody else.

That doesn't leave much for you, does it? Hey, I leave
you a guest room. I wish I could leave you a house in
a place that would make both of you truly happy. But

162

that's something you'll have to work out in your own way.

I also leave you April. Keep on being more than her friend, the way you've already been, if she will let you. And if you can keep in touch with him, be Zack's friend, too. In my place.

You understand you weren't to blame for anything that happened, don't you?

What I feel for you is so deep, I can't

So I don't know what else. I am not scared or anything. Whatever is next is bound to be an improvement. You taught me to expect good things. The best. It hurts me to think you'll grieve and stuff if this turns out sad. But that's part of it. It's supposed to hollow you out to hold the joy, somebody said.

I've had such a good life. Thank you.

So kisses and hugs. I love you.

Jackie

Something has changed.

I am very neat. Lipstick. Hair combed. Bandage on my leg from raincoat lining. Typewriter in lap. Staring up at the spot where the little thin line of light is glowing, like hope.

I thought I would be calm. But inside I'm ticking away. I'm listening to myself be alive.

Yes? Yes.

I am not used up yet.

Are you listening? I'm in charge here. You can't finish me off until I say so.

What is going to be on the next page?

You would love this story, Miss Flannery. Classic mystery. Enough suspense to kill you. But actually it's the same kind of suspense people live with every day, without realizing it, right?

We couldn't live on the edge like this, hour by hour,

if we were aware, could we? Wouldn't it be too intense? We need to chug along believing the sun will rise, water will come out of the tap, and our days will go on ordinary and forever.

I trust you, life.

It's so beautiful out there. I think maybe what I'm hearing isn't my heart plopping and my ears roaring — it's the world vibrating in me. With energy so strong it doesn't even miss a beat as we come and go.

I feel like a gift. Expectant. Sitting in the box, waiting. Who gets me?

Did you feel the same way, Gillie, in the box behind the couch on Christmas morning? Were you as scared as I am? When you felt the box move, and the lid come up, were you ready for whatever it would be? Ready for light, and my hands reaching in to lift you up?

I loved you.

Could you feel it? I can feel it, all around me.

So expectant.

Something is very close. Will I hear my name called? Are cars getting closer? My detective coming? It's up to you, now.

When I was little I would stand by the road as it got dark, waiting for my dad. Such a long time. I thought he wouldn't come. Then finally a little far-off engine sound would start to grow, and I could tell it was going to be him.

So hard to wait.

165

Found myself trying to go up steps on my knees. Get closer to light I guess. One last time? Upset box lid with TTM journal in it. Flipped all little unmailed thinkings down steps and on floor. Scattered. But won't make any difference, if I'm never found, right? And if I am, can put them back in order, to make some kind of sense.

the end